I0581429

Lost in a Nightmare

Jess Charle

Lost in a Nightmare

Jess Charle

Cover Design: Joshua Feliz

Reviewers: Julia O'Connell and Jonathan Harbaugh

Author Photo: Alexander Wozniak

Special Thanks: Josiah Robinson

ISBN-13: 978-1-7376819-0-8

Printed in USA

This book is dedicated to my parents, whose boundless support I have leaned on throughout my life.

While many of the parents depicted in my stories are ugly and cruel, my real parents have always been beautiful and kind and our relationships are full of laughter, love, understanding, and acceptance.

To Jim and Bonnie. Thank you for reading my dark stories since I first learned to write, and sorry for all the judgment you have received because I like to write about wicked parents.

Contents

The Cupid in the Psychiatric Ward

Herman was admitted 3 years ago to the state psychiatric ward where I work as a nurse. No one knows where he came from or who he is, only that he claims to be Cupid.

I was quite fond of him and I'd make a point to visit with him every day. We played chess and he would recite Plato's Symposium to me. I listened to him talk about romance and love and found comfort in his optimism.

I never believed him of course. The notion was preposterous.

That is until a few days ago.

Dr. Josie Griffith was a very plain woman. Her dull brown hair hung limply at her shoulders, her matching brown eyes half-hidden by drooping eyelids. Loose pantsuits draped awkwardly from her body and the building's dry heat created a crown of constant moisture that kissed her hairline. Her thin dry lips turned down at the corners, making even her smiles appear forlorn. She would be forgettable if her plainness weren't so distinct.

She worked mostly with Dr. Wilson and together they made an odd pairing. Dr. Wilson, or Ted, was quite handsome. His brown hair was cut stylishly, the sides shaved neatly while the top section rested perfectly coiffed above his forehead. The dark brown strands were flecked with silver, giving him a sense of maturity. His features were defined but soft, his wide-set eyes shining with an intelligent intensity. He was of average height, maybe a bit on the shorter side, while Josie was quite tall. She loomed above him by almost a foot, emphasizing their stark contrast.

"I'm going to set up Dr. Griffith and Dr. Wilson," Herman said with a wink. We were playing chess and I was three moves away from checkmate.

I looked up, queen in hand, and chuckled. "That's a bit of a stretch, don't you think?" I placed my queen next to his bishop.

He shrugged. "Love works in mysterious ways. I am but its humble servant. Its messenger." He slid his bishop in front of my queen.

Herman was a short chubby fellow with rosy cheeks. My guess was that he was in his early to mid-twenties, but his face still held a youthful glow and roundness that implied he could be even younger. Baby-faced, as they say. His light blond hair draped around his face in tight ringlets and his maroon lips always looked wet, which I found off-putting. He was not an attractive person.

One of the other nurses, Mindy, always made fun of him, saying that the god of love should be more fuckable. Mindy was far from unfuckable or plain. Her shiny black hair was always styled in large loose curls that framed her heart-shaped face. Her ruby red lipstick and prominent widow's peak made her look like a retro bombshell, her curvy frame obvious even in her shapeless scrubs. Despite her beauty, her gnawing insecurities manifested as vicious insults and unfair judgments. She turned her self-hatred and doubt onto others, picking them apart piece by piece like a recess bully.

I disliked her for other reasons though. My throat tightened and my stomach twisted as I watched Dennis' warm smile widen every time he saw her. He'd stop as they passed each other in the hallway to ask her about her day and tell her that her hair looked nice while I only got a small nod and a polite smile that never reached his eyes.

"Well," I sighed, taking Herman's bishop, "I'll believe it when I see it."

He chuckled warmly as his rook slid across the board, taking my queen. "Checkmate."

I began to notice a change in Josie's behavior two days ago. She was smiling more and her normally heavy footsteps seemed lighter. She glowed with warmth and happiness. I didn't think much of it until I saw her getting out of Dr. Wilson's car yesterday morning as I was walking into the building.

"Black or white?" Herman asked, setting up the board.

I fell into the chair, the leather cushion beneath me deflating with a vibrating sigh that I'd have been embarrassed by if not in a room full of crazy people.

"Herman, Josie and Ted came to work together!"

"Who?"

"Dr. Griffith and Dr. Wilson!"

"Well, what do you know?" He winked at me.

"Herman," I leaned across the table. "How did you...?"

He smiled conspiratorially. "I told you," he whispered, "it's my duty. My purpose."

I swallowed and reminded myself that I was speaking to a human being with amnesia and a literal god complex. I heard a giggle and looked over to see Josie standing with Ted, their eyes locked, their bodies facing each other. He said something, his white teeth a glowing beacon against the yellow of the room. Of Josie. She giggled again and playfully pushed his shoulder. Her normal grey pantsuit was replaced with a form-fitting pencil skirt and a white blouse. She still looked plain but you could tell there was an effort. A confidence that hadn't been there before.

"You know," Herman said. I turned back to face him and jumped, surprised at how close his face was to mine. "I could offer you my services."

I leaned away from him, giving us distance. "Herman, that's inappropriate."

"No, I mean. I can help you with Dr. Turner."

I cleared my throat. "I don't know what you're talking about."

"Sure you don't." He sat back in his seat. "Black or white?"

I couldn't help but stare at Josie and Ted as they ate lunch together in the break room. I sipped at my tea, my sandwich mostly untouched. They weren't even trying to hide it. Josie stole one of Ted's grapes and he said something that made her laugh.

The seat beside me scraped across the tile floor as Mindy sat down.

"Oh my god, can you believe it?" she whispered, staring at the new couple.

I cringed. She was really not the person I wanted to discuss this with. "Love works in mysterious ways."

"Uck, gag," she said, opening up a Tupperware full of salad. "Well, good for Josie, I guess. Not sure how someone with a face like that could get any guy, let alone a hot doctor. But, to each their own." She stabbed a tomato with her fork.

A heavy ball of pity formed in my chest. Josie looked so happy. For the first time since I've known her, her smile looked genuine.

"I'm glad they found each other."

Mindy rolled her eyes. "Whatever."

"Is this seat taken?" Dennis said, gesturing to the open seat beside Mindy. She looked up at him, her lips pursed together in a playful smile.

"Sure," she said, her bitchy tone now replaced with coy amusement.

He sat down and nodded to me. My cheeks reddened and I opened my mouth to say hi, but he turned his attention back to Mindy before I could respond.

"So, Mindy. Any fun Valentine's Day plans?"

Her smile widened. "Why do you ask?"

He shrugged. "The boyfriend taking you out somewhere fancy?"

She laughed. "I was planning on ordering Chinese and watching terrible rom-coms. You know, your typical single girl night in."

A dimple formed in Dennis' right cheek as the corner of his grin widened. "Interesting."

"Is it?"

"Those were my exact plans as well."

"What a coincidence!" She exclaimed. "Maybe we should celebrate a sad and single Valentine's Day together. But," she put her hand up, "only if you like Kung Pao chicken."

He chuckled. "It's my favorite."

I looked from Dennis to Mindy. Back and forth, back and forth. Like watching a tennis match. Before I knew it, words were vomiting uncontrollably from my mouth. "I'm not doing anything!" I exclaimed, much too loudly. I could hear Josie and Ted's whispering die down and I was painfully aware of everyone's complete attention now focused on me. "I like Kung Pao chicken too! I can bring brownies!" The second the words left my lips I wished I could scoop them up and shove them back inside.

Mindy looked at me slack-jawed while Dennis stared down at his lunch uncomfortably. The silence of the room weighed on me as heat rose to my neck and face. Tears welled in my eyes and I stood quickly, my chair falling backwards onto the ground with a crash.

"I have to go!" I yelled, grabbing my sandwich and tea before half walking, half jogging out the door.

I followed my feet to the rec room where Herman sat at his usual table reading a book. He looked up at me, his smile fading as quickly as it started. I sat down heavily, causing the last few sips of my tea to splash up out of my mug with the force.

"I need your help," I said, still buzzing with humiliation and hatred. Tears flowed freely down my cheeks. "I need you to make Dennis love me."

He nodded knowingly. "Of course. Anything for you, Naomi."

"What do you need?"

He looked towards the windows. Heavy metal bars ran across them, leaving lines of shadow and light across his face.

With that, I understood.

"Whatever it takes."

I spent the rest of the day locked in one of the spare offices. By nine, everyone from the day shift had left. I walked slowly and deliberately down the hallway, avoiding eye contact with the few overnight staff members I passed. No one seemed to notice me. I approached Herman's room, my body shaking with nervous excitement.

I swallowed, my hands trembling as I unlocked the door.

Herman stepped out of the room.

"Quickly," I hissed.

He nodded silently and I led him down the side corridor, away from any possible activity. The front door had a series of locked gates, complete with security cameras and a 24-hour guard, but there was an emergency exit at the back of the kitchen. The automated alarm had been disconnected by one of the kitchen workers, allowing them to go on smoke breaks without walking all the way across the building. Meaning all we needed was my key card to get into the employee-only section of the hospital and Herman would be free.

I had spent the day imagining all the horrible things that could happen during our escape, but it was blissfully uneventful. I opened the emergency exit door and turned to Herman, who hesitated.

"Are you sure you want this?" he asked. "Messing with love doesn't always work out like you want it to."

"As long as he doesn't end up with Mindy, I'm happy." My words dripped with every ounce of hatred I felt.

Herman gave me a small smile and hugged me. The unfamiliar touch was shocking. It felt wrong. Violating. The smell of chemicals and sweat filled my nostrils and my stomach seized with disgust.

Finally, he let go and walked out into the night. I watched him disappear before turning and retracing my steps back to the main hall. I grabbed my purse and coat and headed to the front entrance, smiling at the guard as he wished me good night.

I woke up today feeling light and alive. Victorious. I wanted to pamper myself like the protagonists of one of the rom-coms Dennis and I would be watching only a few days from now.

I made myself a breakfast of fluffy pancakes with strawberries and whipped cream, followed by a mud mask and mimosas. I sat in the warm bathtub, sinking into the cool porcelain as the scent of steamy lavender surrounded me.

My cell phone rang and I leaned over the side of the bathtub to see who it was. It was the hospital. I wiped my hand on a towel and hit accept.

"Naomi, it's Elijah."

"Um, hi," I said awkwardly. Elijah was the office manager for our ward and he'd only be calling me if it was an emergency. Like a patient escaping. I swallowed nervously and held my breath.

"I'm sorry to call you on your day off but the circumstances require it." He hesitated. "Dennis was murdered last night."

My lungs began to ache with the breath I was still holding, but I couldn't exhale. It was as if my face was paralyzed.

"Someone broke into his house and…. he was shot through the heart with a hunting arrow. They're looking for the murderer, but…" The phone fell from my hand.

The events of the past 24 hours, the past week, have been running on a loop through my mind. With a sickening realization, I think of releasing Herman from the hospital. Of listening to Dennis and Mindy flirt. Of my outburst. Of Josie and Ted.

Josie and Ted, who had been whispering and giggling. Josie and Ted, who had come to work together. Josie and Ted, who eat lunch together and gush about their love of classic literature. Who laugh at inside jokes and talk about going to the film noir marathon at the local art house cinema. Josie, who places her hand on Ted's back as she confides in him. Ted, who is always telling us about the funny things Josie says. Whose face lights up when she enters a room.

Herman didn't make Josie and Ted fall in love, he only noticed it happening. He knew what to look for. I had only seen a plain woman and an attractive man and so I ignored their flirting, their connection. But Herman had noticed. Herman, a man who memorizes great philosophers' writings on love. Herman, a man who recites poetry and thinks it is his duty to spread love.

Herman, a man who thinks he's Cupid.

3:00AM

Every morning at 3:00 AM my mind jumps away from unconsciousness and I awake, my eyes trying to adjust to the heavy night around me. My bladder cries and pleads for release. I know now that it is useless to ignore it.

Every morning at 3:01 AM I shift wearily in my bed, rolling towards the nightstand beside me, and reach begrudgingly for my phone. I wake the screen and groan at the time.

Every morning at 3:05 AM my cat, Freddy, hears me and rises from his spot on the couch. He stretches lazily before silently padding through the living room and into my bedroom, jumping on the bed with a heavy, quiet plop. He meows at me and I sleepily reach out to pet him.

Every morning at 3:05 AM I throw my legs wearily over the side of the thick mattress, careful not to wake my sleeping partner. The soft carpet greets my bare feet and I stand. Freddy mews and weaves between my legs as I shuffle to the bathroom, knowing his early morning snack will be next.

Every morning at 3:09 AM I finish, wash my hands, and continue down the small hall past the door to the garage and into the kitchen.

Every morning at 3:12 AM I flip on the lights. I squint in the sudden brightness. My kitchen looks foreign and forgotten in the early hour.

Every morning at 3:12 AM I top off Freddy's bowl and pour myself a glass of water from the tap.

Every morning at 3:15 AM I turn off the light before walking back towards the bedroom. My feet lead me by memory down the hall as my eyes slowly adjust once more to the black.

But this morning was different. While normally I'd be happily drifting back to sleep by 3:19 AM, my bed and comforter warm and inviting, it was 3:17 and I was stopped just outside my bedroom.

My blood turned to ice in my veins and my heart thumped loudly against my rib cage. Something wasn't right. I replayed my trip, from waking till that moment standing still as a statue, listening to my blood rumble through my ears as I tried to pick up any alien sounds around me. I thought through every minute, trying to separate this morning from all the other identical mornings before it, trying to figure out why pure terror was now inching up my spine like cold sharp fingers.

I closed my eyes and visualized my path down the hallway. Something had been off. The hall was so dark and my brain was still heavy with sleep, but I had noticed something. A small alarm had been triggered deep in the back of my skull and I had known that something was out of place. Something was where it shouldn't have been. I had passed something. I had seen something.

Sweat beaded along my forehead as I turned, slowly, back towards the kitchen. My senses cleared and I could faintly hear Freddy greedily chewing over his bowl. Freddy. Surely Freddy would've been acting differently if there was something off?

I took a hesitant step forward into the darkness, too far now from the hall light, which sat on the other side of my bedroom door, to utilize its comfort. I was painfully aware of the loud creaking that each of my footsteps made against the old wooden floor. I reached the hallway and turned slowly towards the garage door.

The door to the garage was closed. There was nothing out of the ordinary. Relief washed over me. It had just been my imagination.

I laughed out loud at my own foolishness and walked back to the bedroom. I crawled in bed and grabbed my phone once again off of the nightstand: 3:23 AM. I placed my phone back down, not bothering to turn off the screen, and closed my eyes as I rolled onto my back. I breathed in, stretching my limbs out under the cool sheet, relishing the four hours I had to continue sleeping.

My mind began to drift when it came to me. There had been something off. My heart stopped. I could see it now, clear as day. The garage door had been opened before. There had been something in the shadows. Something a more alert mind would've seen right away.

My eyes shot open. The bedroom was softly illuminated by the light of my phone screen and there, standing in my open closet outlined by the doorframe, was a tall, gaunt man. His white, ghostly face was barely visible in the dim light. He stared at me and I stared back, my eyes locked on his dark gaze. He looked lifeless, staring at me without fear or concern, his expression completely blank.

My phone screen dimmed and the room fell into darkness.

My Brother's Sweet Sixteen

My family doesn't celebrate sixteenth birthdays like most. My father told me once that it started long ago, with his great great great great great (etc) grandfather. Way before the Civil War, before our family came to America before there even was an America to come to.

There is a logic, a very old logic, that at sixteen a boy becomes a man, and thus must prove himself as one. And so, to prove themselves, the day before their sixteenth birthday the boys in my family are hunted by their fathers. If the father catches the son by midnight, the boy is killed. If the father doesn't, the boy lives and is forever referred to as a man. They claim it is to ensure that the next generation is stronger than the previous.

It is archaic, but it is tradition. It is our tradition.

I am 14, and I am a girl, so I'll never have to partake of this tradition. My mother says I should be thankful. In four years I will turn eighteen and I can leave this home and never look back. I can marry someone who is unaware of my family's traditions and I can be free. Even if I have a son, he will not have to be hunted like prey.

One night after a big meal and several shots of strong vodka, my uncle told me that when my brother was born, my mother cried for seven days and seven nights. She did not sleep, she did not eat. After the week was over, my father awoke to a deathly silence. She had stopped crying. Father went to my brother's nursery and found he and my mother were gone. He followed her into the snowy night and caught her walking to the village. My mother told him she was going to leave the child at the nunnery.

My father stopped her.

When I was born, my mother wept with relief. She would only have to live the nightmare once.

As my brother's sixteenth birthday grew steadily closer, her crying got worse. She thought I could not hear her at night when my father was out and I was supposed to be asleep, but her pained whimpers echoed off the wooden walls of our house, the thick snow outside amplifying her fear and her future loss.

My father was disappointed in Jacob long before the hunt began. Jacob liked to help mother bake and once even asked her to teach him how to sew. Father ensured that only happened once. A few nights before the hunt, I was serving father and his friends when I heard father laugh that Jacob was already a failure as a man. Father believed he would not survive even the first hour of the hunt. Jacob was not, as my father said, his words wet with phlegm and hate, suitable to continue the family legacy.

My father was a brute of a man, but he was also very cunning. He made his fortune betting against men. He could see weakness deep within their souls. Under hundreds of pounds of muscles and bones, he could see men's hearts and he could judge them. He was very rarely wrong. And he made money off of that judgment. Lots of money.

Mother and I were not allowed to inherit this fortune, and since no one expected Jacob to survive long into the hunt, there was only one man left: my cousin Matthias.

My father told me that if this were 100 years ago, I could marry Matthias and my father's fortune could be ours to share, but marriage of that nature is forbidden in this modern age. So I will marry some stranger with no money to my name. My father will give my husband a modest dowry and my husband will spend it as he likes.

No one ever asked me what I had planned for my future. No, according to my mother I would marry a stranger and be free of barbaric family traditions. According to my father, I would marry a stranger and be at the whims of his finances. My future was a coin flip, if that coin were a two-headed quarter.

This story, though, is not about my brother's hunt, but about how I played the system. My future would not depend on the fancies of men.

My brother came to me the hour before the hunt. He had a bag of supplies mother had given him and the knife father gifted him on his tenth birthday. The hunt does not have many rules, however, the hunting knife was allowed, the supplies from mother were not.

"June," he said, his face taut, "this is for you--a promise." He placed something cold and light in my hand and kissed me on the forehead. "I will survive."

In my palm was a thin gold bracelet. A small pearl hung at its center.

Jacob turned and began to leave.

"Wait," I whispered, rising from my bed. I threw a thick woolen dress over my nightgown--I had already been wearing my woolen tights in preparation--and led Jacob to the front door.

"What're you doing, June?" he whispered through clenched teeth.

"Helping," I said as I pulled on my heavy boots. "Follow me," I hissed as I grabbed my coat and ran outside. Immediately, the falling snow bit at my cheeks and lips. I ignored it and ran.

Jacob often lamented his misfortune for being born in winter. It is easier to track footsteps in winter. He wished he was born in summer like me. But winter has its benefits.

"Where are we going?" called Jacob as he followed. "We should go to the road. It's faster."

"No," I responded, screaming over the harsh winter wind. "That is too obvi-ous. Follow me. The woods have better coverage." I picked up my skirt and began to run faster. Jacob easily caught up to me, his longer legs maneuvering through the white like a dancer's.

I looked up to try and see the color of the sky, to judge how long we had until sunrise when father would begin his part, but the sky was the dull gray of winter, the clouds and snow blocking any sign of how far away the sun was.

"The dark will help us," I told Jacob. "It will slow him down. Give us time."

Jacob nodded as we entered the woods.

The trees sheltered us from the worst of the falling snow, and the snow on the ground was shallower here. I turned to look behind us at our family home. Our parent's bedroom light was on and I could see two figures standing in the window, watching us. I could hear my father cursing in my head, see my mother's tears. The birthday boy was not supposed to have help during the hunt.

But I am tired of having my life dictated by the rules of men.

I spat at the ground as I continued to run deeper into the woods, our home vanishing behind the trees.

I turned back and noticed Jacob was staring at me. "Why are you helping me? Father won't be happy. He'll marry you off immediately for this." His tone grew dark, his words quiet, almost lost in the wind, "And I won't be able to stop him."

"No, he won't."

We trudged along in silence for many minutes before Jacob spoke up again. "Where're we going?"

"To the river."

"Ah, we'll head west. To the mountains. Father will think we went east to the village."

I shook my head, "No, we continue north."

Jacob stopped abruptly. "What?"

"We will continue north. It is our best bet." I turned to face him. "Come now, father will be starting to follow us very soon." If he hadn't already.

Jacob began again begrudgingly. "We can't cross the river. It's too early. It won't be frozen."

"It is our best bet."

"No, we should go west towards the mountains."

"There is only death to the west. We will go north. We will win."

"Win?" Jacob's tone was almost amused, "There isn't any winning tonight. Only surviving."

I bit my tongue and continued towards the river. A soft boom echoed behind us. A gunshot. We quickened our pace. We both knew that if we could hear the shot in this snow, it wasn't too far behind us.

"We go north. It is the only way."

Jacob did not respond.

Soon, the sound of our footsteps was joined by the low roar of the river.

"See?" Jacob asked, "The river isn't frozen yet."

We reached the riverbank and stopped. The thick snow ended abruptly at the edge of the water. The river was ten feet wide, the cold water coursing over rocks and fallen logs.

"We gotta go west." Jacob turned and began jogging in that direction.

"No, we must go north. It is the safest path. Father will not cross the river."

"And neither will we."

"We will figure out a way." I started to scan the river for the way to cross, but Jacob grabbed my arm and began to pull me along.

"No, we're gonna fall, and then there isn't any hope for us."

Another gunshot sounded, closer this time.

"How is he so close!?" Jacob yelled, frustrated.

"We must cross the river, come on," I said as I ran clumsily forward. "Look for rocks we can step over!"

We ran together like this, searching. Suddenly, Jacob stopped.

"Look!"

I looked to where he was pointing. A bridge. Not a professional bridge, but two logs cut and placed beside each other. The far end of the logs was between two large rocks to prevent them from rolling. It was fairly clever engineering if I do say so myself. I nodded and we ran forward.

"I'll go first," Jacob said.

"No, let me." I jumped up onto the logs and was a quarter of the way before Jacob could react. I walked confidently over the bridge, carefully sidestepping the mark in the right log where I had scoured a breaking point.

I landed on the other side with a soft crunch and turned to Jacob.

"Hurry!" I said, but it wasn't necessary, Jacob was already walking my way. His steps were slower than mine, unpracticed as they were. Another gunshot sounded, this time so loud father must have been only a few dozen feet behind us. Jacob ducked down, holding onto the logs beneath him, his legs quaking in fear. I could see hot tears running lines of red down his face.

Perfect, I thought. Father used the snowshoes I left out. I had been concerned in his anger at my betrayal that he wouldn't think of them, so I had made sure to place them right by the door before bed. I knew Jacob wouldn't have thought of them. He hated snowshoeing.

"Jacob! June!" My father's voice, angry but sober, flew over the roar of the river towards us.

I smiled quickly to myself as I started yelling to Jacob again, "Jacob, hurry!"

"June! Girl, you're in a world of hurt!" My father was getting closer. Good.

Jacob stood and gingerly took another step forward. Despite the real danger approaching from behind, he was still proceeding slowly across the river. I watched his feet as they approached the breaking point.

Father emerged from the trees, rifle in hand. He aimed it at Jacob's back.

"Father, wait!" I screamed, just as Jacob's foot landed. The right log cracked like a gunshot and Jacob screamed as he began to tumble into the water. I looked up at Father, who stood there silently watching, but Jacob's screams didn't die into the depth below. Wasn't swallowed by the river. I looked down. Jacob clung to the remaining log, hugging it tightly.

I jumped on the bridge and ran over, stance low for balance, my gaze shooting from Jacob to my father at the other side of the bridge. In my father's surprise, he had lowered the gun and kicked off the snowshoes before beginning his own slow pace towards us.

I guess this will do, I thought. I reached Jacob and he looked up at me, face wet with tears and snot. He reached out his hand and I kicked at his shoulder. Jacob cried out in surprise and pain, dropping his hand to cling to the log again.

"What the fuck, June!?" he screamed, his voice cracking.

I kicked his shoulder, again and again, his body hard against my foot as if I were kicking a rock or a piece of ice. I cried out in frustration and paused before I saw it, his hunting knife. The handle stuck out from the sheath at the back of his belt. I lunged for it, flipping the clasp with my thumb. Father was by us now, watching in shock as I lifted the knife above my head and brought it down into Jacob's back.

He screamed in pain and I did it again. I brought the knife down with a sickening squelch over and over, hot blood covering my face, the front of my dress becoming heavy with it until Jacob's arms grew slack and his body slid off the bridge. He hit the water with a splash and Father and I watched as he was carried away, his blood pooling beneath us for only a moment before it too was gone.

Father looked to me, then extended his hand and helped me back to standing.

"What the hell, June?" he asked.

"I killed him. I won the hunt. I've proven myself, haven't I? I am the legacy you never had in my brother."

Father looked at me for several long moments, his gaze searching my face before he bent his head back and laughed, a deep mocking laugh. He stopped and tried to catch his breath as he said, "You have proven yourself an annoyance, like all little girls. Nothing more. Now come, I will not kill you." He turned on his heels towards the end of the bridge.

"On to plan B, then," I said before kicking him in the back of the knee. Father cried out as his knee gave and he fell to his side on the log. "Good riddance to old rubbish." I raised my foot and kicked him in the groin. He began to roll off the bridge but before his large body cleared the side, he reached out and grabbed my foot. I fell to the damp cold wood and my knee cracked as my father's full weight pulled against my foot. I saw red as pain exploded like fireworks through my leg. I was screaming, my voice high and shrill above the chaos of the river.

Father hung from my dead foot and began to pull himself up, using me like a ladder. Miraculously, I hadn't dropped the knife. I drove it into his arm. The weight on my leg pulled painfully as my father began to swing dangerously below me. I stabbed his other arm and he let go completely, falling into the water. I watched as he was carried away, just like Jacob.

I sat there for several minutes, crying from the pain in my knee, yet still smiling. I had won.

It took me several hours to limp home, but I am a strong girl, and I was able to make it out of the woods before collapsing in the snow outside our house. I was only there for a few minutes before I felt mother's warm arms wrap around me and drag me towards the warmth and comfort of the fire inside. Bolts of electricity shot through my leg as she dragged it through the snow, but I didn't care. It didn't matter anymore.

My mother told the village folk that my father and brother went missing during a hunt, and they were presumed dead. She told my family what she thought was the truth: that my father caught my brother and shot him, but only after Jacob had gotten one good stab to the neck in. This is what I told her happened. I told her I held Jacob as Father bled to death beside us. I did not tell her about the promise bracelet Jacob had given me, or his plans for us, despite these modern times. I did not tell her about how I had spent Jacob's fifteenth year planning how to win the hunt. That I was done listening to the plans of men.

My uncle tried to search the woods for their bodies, but we were blessed with heavy wet snow that buried us. He gave up after several days and told me we would try to find their skeletons in spring. Thank God for lazy men who prefer a fire and alcohol to the truth.

My mother has started planning for my marriage to one of the village men. We need someone to lead the family, she says. Someone to provide for us.

I let her, for now. I told her that she and my future husband can plan the wedding however they like.

As long as she lets me plan the rehearsal dinner.

Synesthesia

My name is Molly and I have synesthesia. I've had it for as long as I can remember.

In case you're unfamiliar, synesthesia is the phenomenon of one sense stimulating another. So, for example, someone with synesthesia can hear colors, or see smells, or taste images.

I see colors when I hear people talk. And everyone's voice is a unique color. My mom's voice is the color of honey. When she laughs, the warm amber thins and shimmers, like honey dripping from a spoon in the morning sun. My dad's is a deep purple, like royalty. When he sings, it turns into a kaleidoscope of different purples and reds. When I was younger, I would lie on the ground and watch the colors play along my ceiling. My sister's is like waves on the beach - a mix of whites and blues swirling and frothing. The more excited she is, the faster the waves rise and fall. When she's mad, the waves are violent and dark, threatening to swallow everyone whole.

My boyfriend in college had a voice the color of cotton candy. Now that I'm older, I wonder if I fell in love with him because his voice was so warm, so promising. It painted a color of freedom and fun, of childhood carelessness. Exactly what I wanted at the time. We lasted for eight months, and by the last month, his cotton candy voice had turned sour and thick like Pepto Bismol.

My fiancé, Ash, is the green of healthy plants. Bright earthy jades mixed with deeper, more robust emeralds. It's ironic because the man cannot keep a plant alive, yet his voice radiates warmth like a greenhouse. It is so strong I can almost smell moist dirt when he speaks.

Like I said, no two people have the same color. Some people's color may be similar, but it's never the same. Even Ash's twin brother, West, is different, if only faintly. He has the same dark greens as Ash, but they are the hues of the deep forest instead of the color of houseplants. His voice resonates with moss, hints of dark wood and humidity throughout. Ash's voice carries an airiness to it while West's is dense and heavy. Ash's family has always been impressed with my ability to tell them apart when even their mother struggles, but all it takes is a loud breath or a sigh, and I can see who it is.

My earliest memory is sitting in my crib, watching my mother and father coo at me. The yellows of my mother swirling with the deep purples of my father, mixing to a rich brown. My mom claims she remembers that day. It was the first time I smiled.

But this story isn't about me. At least, not really. It's my story, but it's about someone else.

It started six months ago.

I was an assistant curator at one of the country's largest libraries. It was my dream job in my dream city. My life was honestly pretty perfect: I was living with Ash in a small one-bedroom in a cute neighborhood with our orange tabby, Nicki. We were so happy, so full of hope.

But like I said, this story isn't about me.

"Molly!" The champagne-colored notes of Becca's voice bubbled and bounced before my eyes. I smiled and turned to face her. Becca dressed as if she worked for a fashion magazine instead of a library. Her blond hair was brushed into a high ponytail, her lips painted a light red that cooled her pale complexion. She wore high-waisted black slacks that accentuated her thin waist with a fitted white button up. Around her neck, she had an orange and red neckerchief.

"Becca!" I returned the excited greeting, my naturally deep tone rising to meet hers. She embraced me and the scent of flowers filled my head, prickling at my sinuses. "There's donuts in the kitchen," she whispered in my ear conspiratorially.

I laughed, pulling away. "Thanks, do you know what the occasion is?"

"New hire," she shrugged, her attention immediately drawn to my pile of books. Her keen eyes skimmed the bindings. "Have you finally jumped off the deep end?" she asked, raising a perfect eyebrow at me.

I rolled my eyes at her, "No, just a new collection I'm intaking." I lifted the book on the top of the pile. The gold letters emblazoned on the cover read, The Role of Conspiracies in Evolutionary Psychology. The book beneath it was Policy and the Bermuda Triangle: How the Devil's Triangle continues to shape US Foreign Policy. "We got hundreds of these books. The guy was a retired professor and he willed us his entire library."

"Fun times," she said as she turned and began to walk away. "Better go get a donut before Carrot Stick sees and lectures you on how eating one of those is worse than smoking a cigarette." The word cigarette hung in the air glittering, even after Becca was out of sight.

The kitchen was a gloomy room in the basement with an old yellowing fridge and a small round table no one ever ate at. This morning, an open box of donuts sat invitingly on the table's surface, a stack of small square napkins beside it. A pink frosted donut caught my eye.

Janice stood by the coffee maker, glowering at the donuts. Like Becca, she was a tall woman, but that was where the similarities stopped. Janice had long silver hair that hung at the back of her neck in a long braid. She wore khakis and a light green sweater, her work ID badge hanging around her neck from a lanyard. She was a stocky woman, her arms and legs thick from the many physical hobbies she told everyone about constantly.

I groaned internally, steeling myself before reaching for the donut.

"You know," the metallic silver of Janice's voice filled my vision and I gritted my teeth, "just one of those has a quarter of the saturated fat recommended for your daily intake?"

My fingers grabbed the donut and I looked at her. "Oh?"

Janice nodded enthusiastically. "That thing," she spat out the word, pointing at the pink offender. The silver of the word "thing" was like a knife, "Is worse for you than a cigarette!"

I am not a fat person. But I am definitely not a thin person and this seemed to offend Janice to her core. I did not like Janice. I stared at her for a moment before bringing the donut to my mouth and taking a large excessive bite, all while maintaining eye contact with her.

Janice grimaced and turned away, carrying her cup of tea with her. "You'll regret that one day."

"What?" I called after her, my smiling mouth full of donut.

"Molly!" The turquoise and goldenrod of Mitch overwhelmed Janice's lingering silver as the large muscular man filled the doorway. "Just the person I was looking for!" Mitch stepped into the kitchen, revealing a much smaller man behind him. The man was unfamiliar to me. The new guy, I realized.

Mitch waved a massive paw at the man, "This is Atlas! He's filling in for Delaney while she's on maternity leave! We meant for Delaney to train him, but…" He trailed off. We had all received the late-night email from HR. Delaney had been rushed in for an emergency c-section weeks before her due date. She and the baby were fine, but it was scary and it left her role unaccounted for since Mitch hadn't found a temp yet. Mitch sucked air through his teeth, an annoying tick of his, before continuing, "I figured he could help you intake that new collection as he gets situated."

I nodded while desperately trying to swallow the dramatically too large mass of half-chewed donut in my mouth.

"Great!" Mitch said, his azure-green-gold voice was constantly filled with enthusiasm. He patted Atlas on the back, the force pushing the man towards me.

I finished swallowing the donut as I reached out my hand to him, "Hi, Atlas! Nice to meet you!"

Atlas smiled at me as he met my hand. He had a friendly if somewhat generic face. He was a young man, about my age, and he had tidy brown hair. His eyes were a similar brown, and he even wore a brown tie with his button up shirt and tan slacks. I wondered if he would sound brown.

"Nice to meet you, Molly. I look forward to working with you. Mitch has been singing your praises all morning."

My smile stiffened as an icy fist grabbed at my stomach. I tried to swallow, tried to look away from those brown eyes, tried to let go of his hand, but I was frozen in place. This man, Atlas, had no color. His words were just that, words. Naked and alone.

"Great!" Mitch said, patting me on the back before turning to walk away. "Keep me posted on how it goes!"

Atlas chuckled as he tried to pull his hand away, "You okay there, Molly?" Mitch's turquoise came and went with him, yet Atlas' words were still blank. Empty.

I stammered as I tried to find my voice, previously the only colorless voice I had ever heard up till this point (though when I watch videos of myself or hear myself on a recording, my voice has a slight pleasant creamsicle color). "Oh, uh, sorry. I just… I-uh-just remembered, I…" I searched my mind for an excuse and came up with "I, uh, I-I forgot to feed Nicki."

"Excuse me?"

"My cat!" The volume of my voice was too loud as I finally let go of Atlas' hand and ran past him towards the women's room.

Silver words followed me into the bathroom: "That's what happens when you don't treat your body right!"

My hand shook as I reached towards one of the bathroom faucets and started the water. I splashed the icy liquid on my face, my breath still catching in my throat, my thoughts racing.

How could someone be colorless? What did it mean? I've seen colors in people's voices since I was born, and no one has yet to be colorless. Someone's color was their soul. Was Atlas soulless? How? Why?

I wiped my face off with a paper towel and steadied my breathing. I was making a bigger deal of this than necessary. Maybe this is his color? Clear. Clear is a color, right?

I inhaled deeply and nodded to my reflection. Clear is a color. I examined myself. My round cheeks were white with splotches of bright red, my brow sweaty. I looked as if I had just finished a run. I inhaled again and let the breath out of my mouth as an "ahhh," like they taught in yoga. It helped, I think.

I tossed the paper towel in the bin, threw back my shoulders, and left the bathroom.

Atlas was standing in the hallway, deep in thought as he read the flyers on an often forgotten bulletin board.

"Atlas, I'm so sorry!" I said, smiling the most genuine smile I could muster.

He turned and smiled at me, "No worries! Were you able to figure out your cat situation?"

"My what?"

His eyebrow rose slightly, "You said you forgot to feed your cat?"

I laughed, the sound tight. "Oh, of course! Yes, I called my fiancé and he said he'll take care of it."

Atlas smiled a warm smile, "Good, glad you were able to get it taken care of."

The day passed as expected, all things considered. Atlas and I spent most of the day working through the collection. I thought maybe I'd get used to his colorless voice, but I never did. When he talked, it was as if death itself was talking to me: cold, lonely, inhuman.

When I got home, I immediately took a hot shower and tried to wash away the chill that Atlas had burned into my joints.

The steamy bathroom filled with the lush greens of a garden as Ash opened the bathroom door.

"Hey, love! Just letting you know I'm home. Rough day at work? Or did you just feel like a post-work shower?"

My tension softened further as the fresh green of his words surrounded me. It was as if today and Atlas was all a bad dream. I thought of telling him about Atlas, about his naked words, but even as I thought of it, my tongue grew heavy and sore from the emotion, the back of my throat closing. I inhaled the steamy green air, and exhaled, most of the stress dissipating.

"I had to train Delaney's replacement today…" I trailed off, "odd guy."

"Yeah? Was he like, creepy or something?" The earthy green turned slightly darker as protectiveness entered Ash's normally jovial tone.

"No, nothing like that. Just… odd."

"Ok, well at least it's temporary. Did you want me to order something for dinner? Chinese?"

I smiled. "Yeah, that would be lovely."

"Sounds good! I'm gonna get your usual, so if you object, speak now or forever hold your peace."

"Perfect."

The next day, I walked up the old narrow stairs to my station, coffee cup in hand, ready to take on the day. Ready to take on Atlas.

As I walked through the second-floor door, I saw him putting books on a shelf. Today he was dressed in a more modern outfit, yet still, it reeked of brown: tweed trousers with an off-white button up. He had done away with the tie - probably realizing that the library was a much less formal workplace. I threw my shoulders back and prepared myself.

"Morning, Atlas."

He turned and smiled at me. On anybody else, it would've been a pleasant smile.

"Good morning, Molly!" His voice was singsongy, yet his words remained colorless. Bare.

I smiled a tight-lipped smile before joining him.

We worked in blissful silence for several minutes, though his presence weighed heavy on my mind. He was a small man, yet he felt like a giant beside me.

"Molly!" The champagne word danced around us, cloaking Atlas. I smiled, relieved, and turned to greet Becca.

"Becca!"

Becca was dressed in a loose red blouse tucked into a sleek beige pencil skirt, high red pumps, and a string of pearls tying the ensemble together flawlessly.

She stood beside Atlas, her color and beauty contrasting starkly with this bland, brown man. Becca eyed him up and down before extending her manicured hand.

"You must be Atlas, I'm Becca. I work in Communications & Marketing."

"She updates our social media," I added, smiling teasingly at her. Becca's presence was so loud and distracting, I almost felt like it was a normal Friday and Atlas was a normal man.

She rolled her eyes at me and turned back to Atlas, smiling. "I also plan events for the library and organize all our print materials."

"Wow, that sounds like fun! What kind of events?" His barren words cut through Becca's warm pearly ones like a knife, leaving the air around us as colorless as he was. I frowned, but Becca didn't notice. She smiled at Atlas, her hand lingering on his a moment too long before dropping back to her side.

"Oh, well we're currently doing a film discussion series! It's so fun! There's a screening tonight if you'd like to join us. We have a lecturer coming from…"

I stopped listening as I watched with disgust as the two conversed, Becca's beautiful colorful words would rise up with her excitement only to be weighed down and drowned by Atlas. Atlas nodded enthusiastically at her words and I groaned internally.

"Atlas, that's such an interesting name!" Becca said, laughing. "Is there a story behind it?"

The man blushed, obviously taken with her. "My mom is a huge fan of Ayn Rand, and she always told me that Atlas was a name of strength. The name of a leader. And that's who she wanted me to be, you know? A leader of men."

"But not women?" I asked, my tone flat. I hated Ayn Rand with the same passion that she hated everyone else. The woman was a pro-"alpha" male capitalist at the detriment of anyone who wasn't a handsome, stubborn, egotistical, up-his-ass "artist" who would destroy things of beauty, women included, to get his way.

Atlas laughed at this comment but didn't respond. This reaction from him made Becca's eyebrow raise and I sighed with relief. She was too smart not to see through him.

"Anyway," Atlas continued, giving Becca a warm smile, "I'd love to join your movie night tonight. What time does it start?"

"The intro starts at six, but we can always use help setting up at five. I'm ordering pizza for the staff."

"I'm in." Atlas smiled, his words sinking into my flesh like acid.

I grimaced, but no one noticed. I had agreed to help Becca set up for the event, and now it seemed I'd have to spend even more time with Atlas. Becca laughed, touching his arm, before turning and beginning to walk away.

"See you two later!" The champagne notes popped above my head, their usual warmth gone.

I glared at Atlas as he walked around the library's event room later that night, his arms full of white plastic folding chairs. He smiled at Becca as he began lining up another row.

Becca beamed at him as she half-listened to Mitch, who didn't seem to notice, his hands enthusiastically flailing as he spoke. My eyes narrowed as I continued to set out the bags of popcorn.

Movie night went well. The presenter Becca hired did a good job guiding discussion after the film ended and there was actually a decent crowd. The presenter's dark red and olive voice mixed entertainingly with the crowd's rainbow of hues. It was one of the more successful movie nights, yet I could hear the emptiness of Atlas' voice even though he didn't say anything during the event. The lack was in his breath, his sighs, his laughter.

Becca came up to me as I was helping clear away the leftover snacks. Her voice was high and giddy, the champagne bubbles dancing around her. "Atlas, Mitch, and I are going to grab a drink next door. Want to join us?"

"Ugh, not if Atlas is going." I angrily swept some loose popcorn into the trash can beside the table.

"Jesus, Molly! What is wrong with you lately?" Becca's champagne bubbles began to pop between us.

"Look, if I tell you, do you promise not to make fun of me?"

Becca's tone changed from frustration to sympathy. "Of course not! What's going on?"

I glanced over at Atlas, who was laughing with Mitch across the room. "It's his voice… he doesn't have a color."

Not many people knew about my synesthesia, but I had confided in Becca long ago.

"Has that ever happened before?"

"No, never. Everyone has a color."

Becca scrunched her face in thought. "Well, you said everyone's color is unique, right? Maybe Atlas is just… unique?"

I lowered my voice further and brought my lips to her ear, "I don't think that's it. Becca, I think he's… I don't think he's human."

Becca's laugh was sudden and loud, surprising me. I shot back away from her. She stopped short and put her hand on my shoulder. "Oh, Molly, I'm so sorry! I shouldn't have laughed, I just wasn't expecting that! I thought you were going to tell me he said something weird to you or you saw him pick his nose or something."

I turned away from her and she put her arm around me, "Oh sweetie," her tone was sickeningly condescending. "Atlas is very much a human, ok? Now come get a beer with us. I'm sure once you hang out with him more you'll get used to him. Just because you don't see a color when he talks doesn't mean he's like… an alien or something."

I pushed her arm away and she sighed.

"Look, his friend Stacey is going to meet us. Maybe seeing him with an old friend will help make you see him for who he really is."

"Fine, I'll go for one beer. But only if you promise you won't date him if I tell you not to."

"Molly, that's unreasonable."

"You can date anyone! Come on, just… just listen to me on this one."

Becca rolled her eyes, "Fine, if it means you'll get a beer with me, then I promise."

Stacey was waiting for us as we walked into the bar. She turned and, upon seeing Atlas, waved, her smiling face glowing with recognition and affection. Relief flooded me. I'm not sure what I was expecting but she looked so normal it was hard to be concerned. She was petite, shorter than me, with a fashionable brown bob, nice jeans, and a loose blouse. I could see her being friends with Becca.

Atlas embraced her in a friendly hug. Maybe Becca was right, maybe I was overreacting. My synesthesia isn't psychic, it's just my brain crossing wires. Atlas let go of Stacey and I reached out my hand to her.

"Hi, I'm Molly."

"Hi, Molly! Nice to meet you!" Stacey grabbed my hand and shook it enthusiastically. I swallowed as her colorless words faded around me. She continued talking but her words were unintelligible behind the rushing of the blood in my ears.

"Sorry, I-I have to go," I said as I turned and left.

I woke up the next morning to 5 missed calls from Becca and several angry texts. I swiped them off of my home screen. It was Saturday. I could ignore her till Monday. I was about to put the phone down and go back to sleep when a new message came in from her.

"You didn't keep up your end of the bargain, so neither did I." There was a photo attached, but I could only see a sliver of it in the preview. I swiped down, revealing the full message. It was a picture of Becca and Atlas at the bar. Becca's eyes were closed, her smile lopsided with booze, her head resting on Atlas' shoulder. Atlas looked completely sober, his smile as cold and piercing as ever. His arm was around her, pulling her towards him.

I groaned and put the phone down, turning over to cuddle into Ash's still sleeping form.

I spent the weekend putzing around with Ash, cleaning the apartment and running errands. Becca never sent me another message after the photo of her and Atlas and I never responded.

Monday came and I took my morning shower with dread heavy in my stomach. I combed the shampoo through my hair and tried not to cry. It'll be ok. I told myself. She's your best friend. She'll get bored of Atlas soon enough and you'll both move on.

I walked through the familiar library hallways, listening for Becca's voice, looking for the champagne words. But I didn't see her. Not in the kitchen, not in the stacks. I even walked by her office despite it being out of my way, but she wasn't there.

I didn't run into anyone but Gabby at the front desk.

"Have you seen Becca today?" I asked the young attendant.

"Oh, she's around! I saw her talking with Atlas earlier. They seem to be getting pretty close." Gabby smiled at me knowingly, too young to wink but the smile was enough to convey her meaning.

I ignored her, "Oh, ok. I guess I just keep missing them. Thanks!"

I grabbed a box of returns from her and went to the shelves to start shelving. It wasn't my job, but if everyone was hiding from me, I'd return the favor.

"Hey." The word hit me by surprise. I jumped and turned to face Becca. "Look, I'm sorry about Friday night, ok?" My stomach was tight, my breathing shallow. Becca looked normal, her hair tied in a delicately created messy bun, her black pants pressed, her sweater clean and perfect. But her words were naked. No, more than naked. Her words were empty. Colorless. The champagne glow gone. Stripped away.

"Becca, what happened to you?" I asked, taking a step back away from her.

She laughed incredulously. "What are you talking about?" Her tone, her inflection, her laugh - everything sounded the same, but I knew. I knew she wasn't Becca.

"Get away from me!" I cried as the world around me became blurry. I remember throwing the books waiting to be reshelved at her. I remember running. I remember calling Ash. Then I don't remember much. I remember someone telling me I needed help. I remember being told I'm confused.

They have me locked in here now. They say it's for my own good. Becca and Ash visit often, asking me how I'm enjoying my spa holiday. They don't acknowledge I'm a prisoner in this oversaturated, overscented hellhole. Ash continues to try to plan the wedding with me for when I'm "better." He's been hanging out with Becca and Atlas. They've been his "support." They're "helping" him. He's never seen Becca so in love with anyone before. He's so happy for them. Becca says she's excited to be my maid of honor. That she and Atlas are moving in together. But where their words were once green and champagne, now they are hollow nothings.

One of the doctors told me synesthesia can fade with age as if that explains it. Why then do I still see his lollipop green voice and the nurse's creamy topaz? How then is it only those who spend time with Atlas who lose their color?

I don't know what Atlas has done with my best friend and the love of my life, but the second I get out of here I'm going to find him and I'm going to make him tell me everything in his colorless, empty words.

Finding Hazel

I buried my face in Hazel's shoulder. Her skin was soft and warm. I inhaled deeply, filling my nose and lungs with her scent. She smelled like… well, she smelled like Hazel. But she also smelled like honey. And coffee. And a little like body odor, but I loved her smell. I inhaled again.

"Are you…" Hazel giggled as she squirmed under me, "are you smelling me?"

I looked up at her amber eyes and smiled. "I like your smell."

She rolled her eyes and scoffed, but her smile remained. I hugged her back into me and smelled her clavicle before kissing it gently. I loved her collarbones. I loved her chest. Her breasts. Her eyes. Everything. She was so perfect. I couldn't believe I was allowed to touch her, kiss her. I couldn't believe she was in my bed. I kissed her neck and looked into her eyes. They were so warm, so full of affection.

She smiled down at me, "Hi."

"Hi," I answered, before kissing her deeply.

I lounged on the couch, bathing myself in the warm spring sun that leaked through the window lazily. Hazel came in and sat a cup of coffee, some toast, and eggs in front of me.

"I made breakfast!" She smiled at me, proud of her accomplishment. Her tank top hung loosely around her bare chest. Her long dreads fell against her back and her shorts revealed her lean muscled legs, covered in tattoos. I reached out and touched her knee, then rubbed up her thigh.

"I'm not really hungry anymore…" I looked up at her as I moved my hands towards the button on her shorts. She smiled coyly, letting me linger, before pulling her hips back.

"Later," she mewed. She walked back to the kitchen to grab her plate, "Food now, sex later." I groaned and grabbed my plate. It did look good and my stomach grumbled at the smell.

My dreams twisted in my mind as I slept. Dark figures and metal probes. I could feel a dull ache in my chest as I tossed and turned. "Keep her under." The voice said as the ache grew sharp. I bolted upright in bed, breathing hard. I closed my eyes tight. It was just a dream, it was just a dream. I forced my breathing to slow and clenched my eyelids. It was just a dream. I opened my eyes slowly and looked beside me at Hazel's sleeping form. Her chest rose slowly, then fell. Relief washed over me.

My biggest fear is waking up to find out Hazel was all just a dream. I can't believe I am deserving of someone so wonderful, so bright and sweet and deep. I kissed her cheek but she didn't react. I smiled wickedly as I straddled her. Her groans turned to moans as I began kissing her neck.

The next day, we decided to visit the zoo. Hazel loved animals and she wanted to see the monkeys. I watched her face light up as we got to their section and she squealed when one came right up to the glass to examine her closer. I bought us ice cream cones and held Hazel's hand as we enjoyed the sun and the warm air and the walk.

I was excited to see my favorite animal: the capybaras. Giant guinea pigs known for their docile nature and eating their own poop. I let go of Hazel's hand and went to one of those generic "zoo animal food" dispensers so we could feed them together. I turned back, my hands cupped and full to the brim. But Hazel was gone. I looked all around and saw kids and their parents, young couples, but no Hazel.

I shrugged, figuring she got distracted by something and would come back soon, and fed the lazy giant rodents myself. Once the food was gone, I turned and scanned the thinning crowd for Hazel, but she was nowhere. I looked up at the sky, once bright and sunny, now filled with an ominous gloom. It never rained here, but clouds don't lie. I shivered, wishing I had brought a sweater and began to walk back towards the monkeys.

By the time I got to the primate section, I was alone in the zoo. I looked for a worker, someone I could ask to call Hazel over the intercoms, but I saw no one. I checked the bathrooms, the gift shop, everywhere, but there was no one there. Panic started to fill my chest and tears came to my eyes. Where was she? Why would she abandon me like this?

Slow heavy raindrops began to fall from the sky. Not knowing what to do, I left. I cried to myself as I walked the empty streets, my shirt and pants slowly becoming soaked through.

Walking into my apartment, I was greeted with the sweet scent of cooking. I walked into the kitchen and saw Hazel standing over the small oven, wearing nothing but an apron. She looked up at me, a huge smile across her face, but when she saw me, wet from rain, my eyes red with tears, her face fell.

"Janet! Oh my god, Janet! What happened?" She ran to me and wrapped me in a warm embrace. I stood there dumbstruck, shivering against her skin. She pulled back and examined my face. "Janet, what happened to you?"

I opened my mouth to speak but nothing came out. I didn't understand. I couldn't comprehend what was happening.

"My poor Janet! Here, dinner will be ready in half an hour. Why don't you go take a warm shower and get changed and I'll make you a nice cup of tea?" She began to steer me into the bathroom. All I could do was nod as I began to strip off my clothes. Hazel left me to check on dinner and I stepped into the steaming shower. As my skin warmed back up, my head began to clear. Once showered and dressed, I felt a lot better, but I was still confused.

I walked into the kitchen, a cup of tea waiting for me. Hazel turned to me, smiling.

"There's my sweetheart! You look much better!" She placed her hands on my hips and kissed my lips. Her body was so warm, so inviting. I felt myself falling under her spell, but I resisted. I pushed her away, much to her surprise.

"What the fuck, Hazel?" She looked at me quizzically, so I continued. "Why the fuck did you abandon me?"

Hazel stammered, her mouth quivering with my accusation. "What are you talking about? I never abandoned you!" Her voice fell, "I would never abandon you."

"Where the hell did you go then? One second we were going to see the capybaras, the next you were gone and I was all alone!"

Hazel's forehead scrunched in confusion. She stared at me for a few seconds, then began to speak slowly and quietly. "Sweetheart, we didn't go to the zoo today. We went last week. Remember? One of the capybaras bit your finger, so we came home and played nurse and patient?" She reached out and grabbed my hip, pulling me closer to her as she spoke.

I shook my head. "No, I was just there. We had been there all day. I walked home in the rain. Just now. That's why I was so wet!" My throat tightened and the next sentence came out weakly, "You abandoned me at the zoo and I had to walk home alone in the rain."

Hazel shook her head and drew me into her embrace. "Shhh, sweetheart. That didn't happen. You know it never rains here." I returned her hug and looked out the small kitchen window. She was right, the sky, while dark with dusk, was clear.

"What the fuck." I said, quietly. What just happened. Hazel shushed me and brought her mouth back onto mine. I sunk into her, letting the fuzzy feelings wash the unpleasantness from my mind.

The dreams came back that night. I could feel electricity running through my limbs. I could hear the voice, yelling. Scolding. She was pissed. "What do you mean you can't increase her dosage. She's waking up. Get her under control. Now." A sharp pain, like a knife, dug deep under my rib. I screamed, the dark cement room around me spinning as the pain grew deeper and deeper. I could feel something close to my ear. It was the voice. Her lips almost brushed my ears as she said "Shhhh, it's ok Janet. Go back to sleep. Shhhhh." It was maternal but wrong. I screamed as another sharp pain entered my right shoulder.

"Janet! Janet! Wake up!" My eyes shot open. Hazel was above me, shaking my shoulders, her face stricken with panic. I swallowed the night air deep, like a swimmer who was under the water for too long. My heart was pounding in my chest, which still ached dully. I rubbed my shoulder, sore from the dream. Hazel wiped my cheek and I realized I was sobbing. "Janet, Janet, are you ok?"

I nodded and grabbed her, embracing her tightly. Hazel held me as I kept sobbing into her shoulder. We lay there in the bed, entwined in each other for hours until I cried myself back to sleep.

In the morning, Hazel acted as if nothing happened. She never asked me what I dreamt about at night. She was such a morning person. Always up and about before me, always chipper. For breakfast, she made French toast with blueberries, which I happily stuffed into my face.

We went to the park that afternoon. Hazel brought a picnic blanket and a basket full of food: brie, bread, grapes, olives, hummus, pita, and more. I laid my head in her lap and she stroked my hair as she read aloud to me. I was hypnotized by her voice, her strokes lulling me into a peaceful trance. I was warm and comfortable. Truly happy.

It took me a minute to realize that Hazel had stopped reading. I opened my eyes and looked up into her deep brown ones. She was smiling at me.

I returned the smile, squinting slightly up at her from the sun. "Hi," I said.

"Hi," she replied. She bent down and kissed me lightly. She pulled apart but kept her lips hovering a few inches from mine. "I love you, Janet."

My heart leapt and butterflies filled not only my stomach but my entire being. I reached my hand up to the back of her head and pushed her mouth back to mine, kissing her long and deep. We broke apart slowly and I looked up at her, "I love you too, Hazel." She kissed me lightly, sat back up and continued reading. I couldn't suppress my smile as I closed my eyes again and allowed her voice to lull me back into a trance.

I woke up with a start. I sat up and looked around. I was still in the park, on the picnic blanket, but Hazel was nowhere to be seen. I stood and searched for her, then looked up at the sky. It was grey again and a cold wind blew past me. The park was empty. I picked up the blanket and the basket and began to wander, calling Hazel's name.

A crack of thunder, louder than anything I had ever heard before, sounded above me and startled me. I wrapped the picnic blanket around my shoulders, the wind growing colder. I shivered as I called louder for Hazel, tears filling my eyes. I began to walk towards the park's entrance when the ground shook violently beneath me. I fell hard on the grass, hurting my shoulder. I cried out in pain and looked up. Rain began to pour in heavy sheets around me. The ground shook again, tossing me into a large boulder.

I screamed as I felt something hit my ribs hard. Another crack of thunder sounded and I could hear the roar deep in my skull. I looked around and I saw her, Hazel, standing off in the distance. She was reaching towards me. I screamed her name and tried to stand, but my legs felt as if they were bound. I reached to her, my vision blurry with rain and tears. Hazel took a step towards me, then disappeared.

I screamed as I closed my eyes tight to try and clear out some of the water, then opened them again. But the park no longer existed.

I was back in the clinic. Dr. Shawl was yelling at someone. Sharp probes were boring into my shoulder and chest. I screamed as a burly orderly kept my shoulders still. I kicked and tried to bite him, but my limbs and head were bound to the table.

"Hazel! Hazel!" I screamed her name, my throat raw from the strain. I was crying, I could feel my face wet with tears. The room around me became calm.

Dr. Shawl pulled the orderly off of me. "It's over," she said sorrowfully. The orderly nodded to her and stepped back. I let my body fall to the table. Pain shot through my shoulder. Dr. Shawl, noticing my clenched teeth, turned to the nurse, "Remove the pins."

I felt pain as the nurse lifted my shoulder and pulled out the large metal pin that had been deeply embedded in my flesh and muscle. She did the same to the one under my ribs and then began removing the sticky pads that connected me via a flow of long colorful wires to an assortment of humming machines that lined the room. Soon, I was naked of technology, lying on the table in nothing but a medical gown and restraints.

Dr. Shawl walked to my side and placed a gentle hand on my shoulder. "Are you ok, Janet?"

I nodded, slowly.

She smiled a small, sympathetic smile. "Do you remember where you are?"

I nodded again. I was in the sleep clinic. What most people referred to, some affectionately and some with suspicion, as artificial heaven.

Dr. Shawl began undoing my restraints. I realized she was talking and tried to focus on her words.

"Less than one percent of subjects are unable to stay in rest permanently. I'm so sorry, Janet. Of course, because of the contract you signed, we can't give you a full refund, but I'll see that you're awarded enough to start your life back in…" she searched for the appropriate phrase, "back in the real world."

I shook my head, tears flowing freely down my cheeks. The restraints were now gone, but I couldn't stand. I didn't want to go back.

"Please…" I begged, snot flowing from my nose. "Please… try again. Put me back under." My voice sounded foreign to me, cracked and small. "Please don't make me leave."

"I'm so sorry, Janet." Dr. Shawl said, nodding to the orderly who came and began to lift me off of the table.

My bare feet hit the cold, dirty street. Tears welled up in my eyes as I looked up at the grey polluted sky. The air was heavy with smog, human coughing and wheezing, and the constant hum of motors. Hazel was gone. She had never existed. I was alone. I was abandoned by computer code. But it was real. She was real. She was mine. I shivered and hugged my bony arms around myself. I squeezed tightly, closing my eyes and remembering the subtle scent of honey and coffee.

"I'm sorry, Hazel. I didn't want to wake up. I swear."

The Angel's Game

TW: See Trigger Warning Appendix

My eyelids were heavy, like sandbags. I forced them apart slowly, using all of my strength to pry them loose as dry crust worked to keep them cemented together. The light around me was blinding. I tried to raise my arm to shade my eyes but both limbs were restrained at my sides.

My tongue was pressed against something wet and soft. I tried to scream but realized my mouth was gagged. Panic shot through my body, my heart pounding deep within my ribcage. Blinking, my pupils began to adjust and my blurry surroundings slowly came into focus.

I was in a small room, illuminated by one light fixture above me, the bare bulb visible below a wide cone of forest green plastic. The wooden walls entombed me, pressing in on each side while the low ceiling hovered above my head. The dark wood was faded and old and the room was completely bare of any art or decoration. My first thought was of an old wood cabin, isolated and alone. Or maybe the mostly-finished basement of an older home. I imagined a suburban family, sitting at their dining room table eating dinner upstairs, surrounded by the faded yellow and brown colors of the 70s while I sat here, bound and gagged below them. Maybe I was to be their Thanksgiving dinner? Flash-fried and devoured, my grease and gristle flowing down their greedy chins, staining the beige shag carpet under their feet.

In front of me was a high table, the surface covered with green fuzz. It was a poker table, my muddled brain realized. Around the table sat three men. In front of me was a white middle-aged man with sandy brown hair and greying temples. His shirt looked clean but rumpled. Washed but not ironed. His face was drawn with age and exhaustion, the face of a boring life spent behind the glowing screen of a computer monitor. He gave the impression of being completely unremarkable. If I ran into him at a store or on the sidewalk, I would forget him instantly. He blinked slowly, his mind not yet comprehending the direness of the situation, a red gag tied around his mouth.

Movement from the corner of the small room caught my eye and I looked to find a short bulky woman with chestnut hair lined with silver leaning against a wall. Her eyes were magnified behind thick-rimmed glasses and a dull crooked knife rested lazily in her hand. She was looking at me. As my eyes caught hers and she smiled idly like a cat whose trapped prey finally noticed the sharp teeth beside its head.

The woman's brown eyes were oddly warm for the situation. If it weren't for the cruel-looking dagger in her hands, she'd look like a librarian or a teacher. But beneath the warmth was something more sinister. An illness, a hatred, masked by years of obedient feminine hospitality and tenderness. She bowed her head slightly in my direction and without thought I returned the gesture.

She pushed herself from her post and stood beside the table. The woman raised her arm and with a flick of her wrist, whacked the edge of her knife against the green shade of the lamp above our heads. The thin chain attached swayed with the force and the light choked and sputtered. The woman grinned, pleased with herself.

For the first time since I awoke, no longer clouded with sheer panic, I heard the voice within my mind speak up, "The fuck?"

"Hello, my darlings!" The woman crooned, raising her arms over her head as if to embrace us in greeting in a caricature of a loving grandmother, the light still swinging above us, shadows growing and shrinking rapidly over our faces.

I looked around at my fellow hostages, searching for answers, but each face I met was filled with the same terrifying confusion that I knew was polluting my own features.

The woman lowered her arms and beamed. "I'm sure you're all wondering why I've gathered you here today. Well, now… that's an interesting story… an interesting story indeed." She took her glasses from her nose and rubbed them between two folds of her pale yellow sweater.

I shifted my arms slightly, trying to gauge my range of motion. My father, a very pragmatic sort of fellow, bought me a small Swiss Army knife for my thirteenth birthday that I always kept attached to my keys. Unless this crazy old woman emptied our pockets, I might still have it. If I could raise my hand just a little bit, I might be able to reach…

"Tsk tsk tsk," I jumped as the woman's low tutting sounded directly behind me. I tried to turn but I was unable to twist my body enough to see her. "Ms.

Christine," she said sternly, still the teacher, the librarian, the grandmother condemning a small child. The "s" sound at the end of Ms was exaggerated, like the hiss of a snake, the warning of a boiling hot kettle. I stopped, my pulse quickening. I tried to swallow but the limitations on my tongue from the gag made it difficult. "Trying to leave our little gathering before even hearing why we're all here?" She lowered her mouth to my ear, her warm breath hitting the side of my face as I felt her lips curl into a snarling smile. She whispered, her voice low, the air vibrating like a small drill boring deep into my brain, "How rude."

My arm slackened. The line of perspiration that had formed on my forehead began to dry as a slight breeze hit me from an unknown source in the otherwise still room. The woman's face lifted and I exhaled. "There will be none of that. I assume the rest of you understand." The men around me looked from one another, unsure whether to be afraid of the situation, the woman, or both. "Are we all ready?" she asked expectantly. We looked at her uncertainly.

"All of you have one thing in common: you must be resolved. Luckily for you, I'm here to help." She smiled at us warmly.

The forgettable man across the table mumbled something, his voice cut off by the gag. The woman smiled patiently at him as if she could understand his question.

"Patience. All will be revealed presently." She walked towards the man sitting to my left and placed a small revolver in front of him. The cold metal fell to the felt tabletop with a small thunk. "All of you have committed a great sin and now all of you must earn your redemption." She cut the bounds on the man's right hand with a swish of her dagger, the edge of which now gleamed red where she had grazed skin. She held the dagger to his throat and explained, "You will all be playing a game of Russian Roulette."

A commotion erupted as the man to my right, a lean white man with a scruffy face and chin-length brown hair, began to yell, the words unintelligible. I couldn't help but realize how attractive he was.

The woman smiled at him pleasantly, her eyes betraying only a hint of disgust. "Please Joe, calm down. There is no need for alarm." The man's forehead scrunched up as he tried to raise his voice but only emitted a jumble of noise. The woman straightened, never removing the dagger from the other man's neck, her face grew stern and a pit formed at the bottom of my stomach making me feel ill. It was a feeling I remembered but hadn't experienced since childhood. That utter fear as a young child when an adult was mad at you. A feeling I hadn't experienced since high school when my mother walked in on me fucking my secret boyfriend. Joe seemed to get the feeling too because he stopped yelling and settled back into stillness.

Satisfied, the woman continued, "There are four of you here tonight but this gun has only three bullets. Each of you will shoot yourselves but only three will die. One of you will leave here unharmed while the others will go to heaven having repented for their sins."

I looked at the woman, stunned by the revelation. I tried to speak, growling my question at her. "And who are you to give us redemption?" I said, but all that was heard was "mmm mmm, mmm, mmm mmm mmmm mmmmmm?"

The woman rested her free hand on her chest in a mocking gesture of faux surprise, "Who, me?" She smiled wickedly, "Isn't it obvious? I'm an angel."

We all stared at her in silence for a moment, stunned by the claim. She continued, "I know you're all probably wondering, 'but wait, isn't suicide a one-way ticket to hell!?!' Very good question my darlings. See, since you do not know whether or not there is a bullet in the chamber when you pull the trigger, that is one sin you will not have committed in God's eyes. A Schrödinger's bullet, if you will." She smiled at us.

I raised an eyebrow at her logic and then looked at Joe, who continued to stare straight at the self-proclaimed angel, fear and hate mixing on his face.

"Because Joe," she said sternly, her eyes narrowing in his direction, "your options are to play the game and go to heaven, or don't play the game and go to hell." The dagger in her hand pressed against her present victim's throat. A smothered cry filled the room and fresh blood beaded against the metal. Whether this woman was actually an angel or not didn't matter. It was clear we didn't have a choice. "Now, no more questions. It's time to play." She looked down, "Ok, Robert. Go ahead and pull down your gag so you may confess."

Robert, his eyes wide with terror, raised his now free hand and slowly tugged at the gag in his mouth, pulling the taut red cloth with difficulty. He groaned with the strain, careful to avoid pressing further into the dagger at his throat. Finally, the cloth gave as it was pulled past his chin and Robert let go, letting it hang loosely, resting on the now-red fingers of the angel.

"Now grab the gun and point it at your head," the angel commanded, her voice cold. Robert's hand trembled as he reached for the gun and brought it to his forehead. The barrel shook against sweaty skin as he stared down at the green table.

"The rules are simple," the angel stated, never taking her eyes off of her first victim. "Introduce yourself to the group, tell them your sin, then pull the

trigger. Die or survive, your soul will be redeemed and you can go to heaven."
She smiled sweetly.

The man nodded his head slightly, avoiding too much movement, and began,
"My name's… my name's Robert." The angel nodded encouragingly. Robert
stared up at us, his throat taut, his eyes pleading. He was a black man in his
late thirties with dark hair, the tight curls cut close to his scalp. He was a
stout man, not particularly muscular but he didn't look weak. His skin was
rich and smooth and he had a look of intelligence about him like he was
an engineer or a scientist. His eyes were outlined with stylish black glasses,
simple and modern. An architect maybe? His arms were thin, but his belly
was beginning to protrude in a slight paunch. I noticed his fingers, clutched
around the gun, were long. Robert, the piano-playing architect? Robert, the
sinning piano-playing architect?

"And what is your sin, Robert?" the angel cooed.

Robert's head twitched to the right, a shake of resistance. The dagger bit deeper into his throat. "What is your sin?" the angel growled as a thin stream of
blood trickled down his neck. A tear welled in the corner of Robert's eye and
his head jerked again. The dagger bit deeper and a grunt of pain left his lips.

Roberts inhaled shakily and started. "I…" his lips trembled with the effort,
eyes upturned towards the ceiling, towards God, tears now flowing freely
down his cheeks.

The angel nodded, speaking encouragingly, "You know what you did."

He sniffled, and continued, "I drink too much."

"And?" the angel asked.

"And I… I sometimes get… too drunk."

"Come now, you know that's not why you're here," the angel answered.

"I.." Robert's eyes filled with tears, the gun quivered against his temple as his
voice shook with the effort of confession. "I… I got too drunk one night and… "

The angel nodded, patting the top of his head with her free hand in what
might have been a comforting gesture if her other hand wasn't wet with his
blood. "Keep going," she hissed between her teeth.

Tears fell from his eyes and a thick glob of snot began to slowly drip from one
nostril. "I… I killed her…" The force of a choked sob stretched his skin into the
blade and he gasped. The snot was now flowing down his face, hovering just

at the edge of his top lip. I watched in disgust as the snot inched ever closer to his open mouth. The felt in front of him was turning brown with blood.

"Why did you kill her?" the angel asked.

"It was, it was an accident!" Robert yelled, his eyes wide with panic, "I swear, I didn't mean to! I just pushed her, she was antagonizing me!" He gulped and looked up at the angel, "She was taunting me!"

"Why was she taunting you?"she asked, her voice rising with anger.

"Because… she… she caught me…" He paused, looking from me, to Joe, to the dull man, begging for help, but all we could do was sit there and watch, waiting.

"She caught you what?" The angel asked, lowering her face closer to Robert's, spitting the words at him with disgust.

"She caught me having sex," Robert said, tears flowing, snot now dripping in front of his mouth, trembling from his shaking breath.

"Having sex with who?" The angel cried.

"Having sex with another man!" Robert screamed. He sobbed, no longer seeming to feel his cut and bleeding throat. His body shook with his pain, "She caught me having sex with my co-worker, Paul. She caught us because I was drunk and stupid and wasn't thinking." He sobbed, "We usually went to Paul's place but we got really drunk and the bar was just down the street from my apartment and I thought she wasn't going to be home till later and she walked in on us and saw us." His shoulders heaved with his cries, snot dripping onto his lower lip. "She… she fucking laughed at me!" Robert cried, furious with the memory. But the fury was short-lived. He immediately sank back into his seat and looked down with shame, "I pushed her, I just wanted to shut her up, but I was drunk and I pushed too hard. She fell and hit her head. She… she bled out. Maybe if I were sober I would've called an ambulance in time. Maybe she could've made it. But… Paul and I freaked. We wrapped her body in the bedroom rug and… and…" He choked again, trying to catch his breath so he could continue, "And then we threw her in my building's incinerator." He sobbed again, "I… I told the cops she'd run away…"

The angel nodded, satisfied, and squeezed Robert on the shoulder. Sniffling, never taking his eyes from the table in front of him, he pulled the trigger.

The room filled with the explosion, which echoed through my bones, reso-nating deep inside my gut. Robert was no longer at the table, the force of the shot pushing him from his chair, which fell on top of him, still attached to his left hand with the angel's rope.

She turned to us, smiling with satisfaction, "Good! Very good! One soul down, three more to go!" the anger and disgust that had been in her voice only moments before now gone completely, replaced with a sickly sweet tone. She reached down, picking up the gun from the floor, and placed it in front of the unremarkable man across from me. With her other hand, she dug the dagger between his face and the gag, causing the man to cry out, and pulled it forward roughly, releasing the cry halfway through so it rang clear above the table. The gag fell away. A thin line of red swelled on the man's cheek where the tip of the knife caught him. My first thought was that his new scar would make him much more memorable. If he survived, that is. The angel sliced the restraints on his arms and placed the dagger to his throat.

He picked up the gun. "My name," he started, hesitantly, "is Marcus."

"And what is your sin, Marcus?" she lingered over his name, letting each syllable fall onto her tongue and pour from her lips. I could hear the satisfaction in her voice, the greed for more.

Marcus continued, his voice low and static.

"Which one?" he asked, his face blank.

At this, the angel smiled wickedly. "You know which sin upsets God the most."

He nodded his head slightly, "Yes, I do."

"Confess," she ordered.

"I murdered my son's wife," he said, simply. He didn't need to be prompted to continue, "She was tempting me, with her flirting, and her...suggestive manner. She wanted me. I knew it. So we consummated our... it wasn't love. It was pure, animal lust." The corner of his lip rose in a half-smile. He was reveling in his sin.

"Why did you murder her?" the angel asked.

"Because she was a dirty slut and I didn't want her to taint my boy anymore." He spat at the thought.

"So you raped and murdered your son's wife?" the angel asked.

The man laughed. It was dark and sharp, more like a bark than an actual human laugh, "You can't rape a whore."

The angel shook her head sadly. "Coveting someone else's wife is a sin, Marcus. You know this."

Marcus nodded and pulled the trigger.

My ears rang with the second explosion and I felt wetness on my face. Unlike Robert, Marcus didn't fall over. His chair swayed with the force before slowly righting itself. His body steadied and there he stayed, in front of me, his head dangling loosely to his chest, part of it now missing. I gagged as a piece of Marcus fell from my cheek onto the table with a damp thud. My body was shaking uncontrollably and I realized I was crying, unable to take my eyes off of his dilapidated skull, my face wet with the warmth of blood and tears.

The angel smiled, looking from me to Joe. "Well that one was short and sweet, wasn't it?"

I looked to Joe, who was pale with shock. The angel bent down and picked up the gun from where it fell. Straightening, she smiled as she walked towards him. She placed the gun down and stepped behind him, her eyes twinkling. She cut his restraint and raised the dagger to his throat, digging it deep into his skin, red trickling down his throat. Her fingers grabbed the red cloth around his face and pulled it down sharply. I could see the scratch marks on his cheek from her nails. "Your turn."

Joe stared at me quizzically, his intense stare burrowing beneath my skin to my core. I shivered, helpless.

"I...I don't know what my sin is."

"I'm not surprised," she said softly. She stroked Joe's hair with her free hand, "Why don't you tell us about your wife."

"Mary?" Joe asked, bewildered. "She...she's dead."

The angel nodded encouragingly to him, though he couldn't see her. "And you're the one who killed her."

Joe's mouth opened with astonishment, his lower lip trembling. "What?! No, I didn't. It was cancer!" he yelled defensively.

"Tell us about that."

Joe stammered and looked down at the table. "A few years ago, she was diagnosed with breast cancer. The doctors thought it was early enough. That they caught it before it got bad, but... no matter what they did, she kept getting sicker."

"Mmm." The angel nodded, "And where were you?"

"I was..." Joe's forehead scrunched in confusion, "I don't know... I was working a lot... trying to make some extra money for her health bills and to keep us afloat... I didn't cheat on her if that's what you're implying."

"Oh, I never implied such a dreadful thing!" The angel cried in mocked offense. She lowered her hand to his shoulder, "I'm just curious as to why you spent your wife's final days at work instead of at home with her?"

Joe shook his head, "I told you, I had to work extra to make money. Her medical bills were extraordinary! I worked two jobs for years to try and make ends meet."

The angel lowered her face to his ear, "And was it worth it?"

"What!?" Joe cried, incredulous.

She straightened again. "Was it worth it? I've seen your debt. I know, even after years of working overtime, day and night, you owe the hospital thousands of dollars. Debt you most certainly will never pay off. I also know you quit your second job once your wife passed."

"I had to plan the funeral! I had to grieve!" Joe stammered, defensively.

"So," the angel lifted her dagger into the air, "you absolutely had to work during your wife's final days," she punctuated the sentence with a flail of the knife, "but after she died, you could quit the second job to focus on yourself and getting things done?" The dagger hung loosely above Joe's head.

"What?" Joe didn't seem to notice the absence of the metal at his neck. His eyes forward but unfocused as the angel's words echoed in his mind. "No. I... I had to work..."

"You didn't have to work. You had to get out of the house. You didn't have to make more money, you were never going to be able to cover those bills, wouldn't it have been better worth your time to spend every last second with your dying wife?"

Joe didn't answer but continued looking straight ahead, eyes glassy.

The angel continued, "Admit it, Joe, you didn't want to be with her. You didn't want to take care of her. You would rather work yourself to the bone than spend one more minute with your pathetic, sick wife. You weren't a martyr, you were a selfish, scared little man."

A large tear rolled slowly down his cheek. Joe sniffled. "It was too much. I couldn't... I couldn't take it." A choked sob forced its way up his throat. He coughed it out, losing all self-restraint, and began to sob.

"Were you relieved? Once it happened? When you found her dead? Was your heart lifted?"

Joe nodded, slowly. He looked and sounded like a toddler who had been scorned on the playground. "I just wanted her to go away. I just wanted to not have to watch her wither away anymore. It was too much."

"You had promised her to be there in sickness and in health, but you didn't realize she was going to get so sick, so soon. You were young, you were stupid, you were a liar," the angel hissed.

Joe reached out and picked up the gun. He raised it to his head, closed his eyes, and pulled the trigger. The gun clicked, the hammer hitting nothing but air. He opened his eyes in amazement, stunned for a moment before relief washed over his face.

"Congratulations, Joe!" the angel cried with genuine enthusiasm. "I'm happy it's you who survived!"

Joe couldn't stop the smile from forming on his lips, his face still red from Marcus, wet from the memories of his dead wife. The smile faltered as his eyes caught mine. The angel noticed and looked to me as well.

"Oh no… well, I want all of God's children to be redeemed in his eyes, so the game must go on. Even if we already have a winner. Because when every soul is washed clean with confession, we're all winners." She smiled at me as she walked to my side and undid the gag and restraints. My arm fell limply to my side, I was numb. "Go on Chris. Tell us your sin." Joe placed the gun in front of me, still sniffling, completely accepting his fate as a pawn in this game.

I blinked at him as the dagger bit into my neck. How could I be here? What on earth had I done that could upset this so-called angel? And then it dawned on me. What all these men had in common. Not that they were disgusting or disrespectful or womanizers. And suddenly, I realized the angel's morality was obvious all along. And with that, I realized what I didn't have in common with these men, born the way they are and happy with themselves and the body this angel's God gave them. "I know what you want me to say. But I won't say it."

She tilted her head quizzically, "And why not?"

"Because it's not a sin."

"Oh, Chris." She tutted at me, her voice dripping with mocking sympathy. "But it is a sin."

My body warmed with anger, my face drying, the tears no longer coming. "Says who?" I spat.

"God," she responded, her voice low, almost a growl.

"Then he isn't my God," I answered, setting my mouth tight with determination.

The cold metal of the dagger, stained with the blood of at least three men, dug deeper into my skin. I inhaled sharply, a hiss emitting from my lips.

"He is your God, Chris," The angel's voice was filled with hate and disgust, "whether you like it or not."

"No," I answered. "He is your God, but he is not mine. My God would not value homosexuality, coveting someone's wife, lying, and being born in the wrong body as worse sins than murder, rape, and abandonment. My God would not value seven stupid rules over treating other humans with respect and decency."

The knife dug deeper, I choked as blood poured onto my chest.

"And," I added through clenched teeth as I picked up the gun in front of me, anger radiating up through me, "my fucking name is Christine."

I remembered the angel's earlier comment: Schrödinger's bullet. The location of the bullet is now a certainty, so no matter what, I'd be going to hell. According to the angel's rules, I'd be screwed either way. I pointed the gun, the weight of the final bullet heavy in my outstretched hand, and pulled the trigger. Joe fell backward with the impact as blood exploded onto the wall behind him.

I had thought about shooting the angel, but angel or not, something in my mind told me I couldn't. Something forced me to play her game, just like it did for Robert, Marcus, and Joe. Something wouldn't let me fight back, only go forward. I don't think it was God, maybe it was survival. Maybe shame. Maybe human idiocy and fear of the potential of God.

I felt the dagger drop from my neck. I placed the gun down on the table and raised my free hand to the wound, pushing against the steady stream of blood. The angel laughed deeply behind me.

"Fucking humans," she said with disdain as she walked towards the door that was behind Joe and opened it. She paused, her body hovering in the dark nothingness that greeted her outside the door. I couldn't tell if it was a hallway, or the outside, or… something else entirely. Turning her head slightly, she spoke one final time.

"See you soon, Chris."

I'm Turning into my Mother

Since I turned 20, it's been happening more and more. I'll open my mouth and an idiom I've heard my mother use time and time again will spill out. I'll watch a movie and become aghast at the provocative nature of the female protagonist. I'll grimace when I notice my friend isn't wearing a slip under her hinting-at-sheer skirt. My friends laugh at the naturalness of the situation, thinking I'm just growing older, adopting the long-held traditions and thoughts of my overbearing mother. The mother who scolds me for frowning, because it'll ruin my smooth skin, or for using the wrong moisturizer or makeup, which makes me break out, or for eating pizza, because it'll make me fat.

Thursday was my 21st birthday. In true newly legal status, my friends and I went out bar hopping on a mission from the gods to get more drunk than any newly 21 years old before us.

I woke up the next morning ill. My head pounding against my skull like a fetus kicking the lining of its mother's uterus. I felt simultaneously nauseous, exhausted, and like I had to take a massive shit. I ran into the bathroom, hoping I could relieve at least one symptom.

Thirty minutes later, I rinsed my face with cool water, relishing the sensation on my clammy skin. I looked up into the mirror and saw her. My mother. It wasn't that I saw her face in the mirror instead of mine. I saw her in my face. The crook of my mouth forming her always present half-smile, the way my eyes were looking up while my head was tilted slightly downward towards the sink, the way my nose was scrunched, the lines in my forehead that met in the middle. They weren't mine, but they weren't foreign. I knew those lines, that scrunch, that look, that smile. It was my mother's. I wasn't adapting the familiar words and expressions and ideals I was taught living with the woman for 18 years, I was her. For a split second, I couldn't recognize myself in my own features.

I called her then, but she didn't answer, her phone drifting lazily into voice-mail. I left a quick message and hung up, then called my boss and told her I was taking a sick day. I forced down some orange juice and went back to bed, to forget about the incident.

That is, until this morning, when I woke up from the first nightmare I've had since I was a child.

I was me but also I wasn't. I woke up in a different bedroom, a room covered in posters and filled with knick-knacks, trophies, and photos that weren't mine. A sloppy stack of albums lay in the corner along with discarded clothes and a white bra. I recognized most of the people in the posters: there was a young Madonna in black lace, Michael Jackson with his fedora covering most of his face, a white-gloved hand on top, and the two curly-haired men from Tears for Fears whose names I don't know.

I lifted the covers and placed my feet on the faded pink carpet. Noises were coming from outside the bedroom door and I followed them, the carpet rough but not unpleasant against my bare feet. There was a full-length mirror leaning against the wall and I stopped to look at myself. I looked to be in my early twenties, wearing a long white cotton nightgown with yellow flowers embroidered along the high neckline. My face was familiar, but also distant. Like another version of me. Like when I looked into the mirror yesterday after my 21st birthday. The chin was soft, like mine, but the blue of my irises was a shade or two lighter and the almond shape of my eyes was wider, the eyelashes shorter and lighter. My brown hair was cut with thick straight bangs, my frizzy wavy hair shoulder length when I usually wear it much longer. My eyes skittered downwards briefly and I realized with jealous annoyance that my breasts were much larger than in reality.

A loud bang sounded outside the bedroom and I opened the door hesitantly. There was a faint acidic chemical smell in the air of the hallway. I followed the peculiar smell to a closed door and opened it.

I was in another bedroom, much barer than the one I woke up in. Sitting cross-legged in the middle of the floor was a woman in her mid-forties. Her brown hair was short, ending right below her ears and she wore a black dress, the velvet sleeves flowing down her arms, covering almost every inch of her porcelain skin. She looked up at me, her blue eyes twinkling, her mouth set in a small, crooked half-smile.

I recognized the woman from old photographs in withered albums in my mother's attic: my grandmother. She sat in a white circle, spray-painted onto the carpet, the faded pink fibers matted together in the sticky white residue. But it wasn't just a circle, it was a pentagram. A star with too many points for my sleepy, bewildered mind to comprehend. It was ornate, swirls and shapes extending from each point, filling the room. Inside the circle in front of her was a large bronze bowl, filled with something that appeared to be sand or dirt.

The smile stayed on her lips, only a whisper of pleasure, as she lifted her hand, an ornate purple bottle between her fingers, and poured a clear liquid into the bowl. The air around us became thick with what I can only describe as an electric charge, sending my hair on end, threatening to crack violently and kill us both. My feet instinctively began to shuffle back towards the door when something struck my chest with a heavy force, knocking me backwards.

I closed my eyes and winced in pain, tears forming on the edge of my eyelids. It felt as if there was a heavy weight against my chest. I opened my eyes and tried to right myself, but I couldn't under the force. The room began to spin around me and I closed my eyes to avoid feeling nauseous.

After a few minutes, the sensation dissipated and I looked up. I blinked as my eyes focused on the figure of my grandmother in front of me. Wait, no. It was me. The me I had woken as. I looked down, my body clad in black velvet. I looked up, heart pounding, as the dream me reached up to the top of the dark dresser against the wall and came back with a knife. She crawled towards me, one knee dragging through the carpet followed by the other.

I tried to crawl back away from her, from me, but I was stopped by the bed. The thought of getting around her and running to the door rose in my mind, but too slowly. She was above me, her hand raised, the knife blade shining threateningly. I looked from the knife to her, the dream me, and as our eyes locked, her face twisted.

Twisted into a crooked half-smile.

I woke up in a cold sweat, my heart racing. I was relieved for a moment that it was just a dream until my doorbell rang. I walked to the front door of my apartment in my sweatpants and an old t-shirt and looked through the peephole. There, standing in the hallway, was my mother. My stomach dropped.

"Sweetheart?" She called, pressing her eye close to the peephole as if it were two-way. "Are you there? You sounded ill on the phone yesterday. I tried to call back and I got worried when you didn't answer!"

She stood back from the door, removing her eye from the peephole, and all I could see was that smile. The smile I had seen moments ago in the most vivid dream of my life.

Real People. Not Actors.

TW: See Trigger Warning Appendix

There's a new car commercial on television, have you seen it?

Unsuspecting real people, not actors, are led out from what is presumably their house to find a brand new SUV parked in the driveway. They ooh and ahh over how pristine and shiny it is, saying things like "this is the most attractive SUV I've ever seen" or "it's so stylish, so modern." Then the spokesperson, dressed appropriately for the late January weather, opens the backdoor and the subject's real family, not actors, pop out like an overcrowded Jack-in-the-Box. Everyone squeals and screams in delight, hugging each other tightly while still finding space in their joyous meeting to coo at the car behind them, as if the surprise reunion and the SUV are now so intertwined they can't help but think of the inanimate object as part of the family.

Now they have to buy it. Now you have to buy it. You wouldn't not buy a member of your family, would you? You wouldn't abandon your family, would you? Only a real animal abandons a member of their family like that. Though I suppose, animals have a sense of loyalty one shouldn't disregard, so only a real sub-animal would abandon their family like that. A real low-life.

You don't want to be a low-life, do you?

Well, I was in one of those car commercials. Sort of. Let me start from the beginning.

My boyfriend, Henry, is an actor. Though the term "actor" is a real stretch. One might be inclined to call him more "real person" than "actor." Ever since I've known him he's wanted to be in front of an audience, despite having no natural acting abilities nor any desire to memorize scripts or practice. I think his logic was that if he pushed the universe enough, eventually he'd be given a spotlight. He was desperate to be famous, even if it was for only a few minutes.

About a year ago he started focusing more on commercial gigs than "real" acting gigs. I guess he figured commercials would be easier.

"Lean against the counter and eat a spoonful of cereal. Act as if your life has meaning now. Do you practice mindfulness? Try to look like you're practicing mindfulness as you eat the cereal."

I was reading a novel in the tub when Henry came bursting in, screaming about how he had done it. I had been fully relaxed in my little ritual of self-care and the outburst completely surprised me, causing me to drop my book in the bath.

"Goddammit!" I cried as I fished the book out from the soapy water and threw it on the floor. It sat there open, the pages melting into the synthetic fibers of the bathmat beneath it, completely ruined.

"I did it! I did it, babe!" He cried, his hands raised in triumph, one clutching his phone as he looked at me, "I did it!." The dimples in his cheeks were deep from the wide smile stretched across his face. He looked almost manic.

I inhaled, the lavender scent of the bath filling my nose as I tried to calm my frazzled nerves.

"What did you do, Henry?" I asked through clenched teeth.

"I got a gig! A gig, babe! A real gig! Isn't that crazy, babe?" Henry had the infuriating habit of saying "babe" constantly as if he were a sheep baaing.

My anger melted with shock and happiness at my partner's joy. I shrugged off the book. Buying another wasn't too much of a hassle and it could have been worse - it could've been my kindle. "Oh my god, that's wonderful!" I stood, naked and wet, and we hugged in excitement, the now lukewarm water lapping gently at my calves.

"And guess what, babe! You get to be in the commercial too!"

My grip on him loosened as my enthusiasm waned. "What?" I asked, pulling away from him.

Henry straightened, his smile engulfing my entire view as he looked at me. "It's a family commercial, babe! They want you too! Isn't that awesome!?!"

"Why can't they cast you a professional girlfriend?" I didn't try to hide the sarcasm in my voice.

"Babe, it's a "real people, not actors" thing, so it's got to be the real deal." His face fell in concern, "You'll do it with me, won't you?"

My heart pained and I sighed, "Of course, love. Anything for you."

Henry cried out in glee, "thank you, Claire!!!" He gave me another squeeze before running out of the room, "I'm gonna call my mom!"

"You might want to change your shirt too!" I called after him as I bent down and pulled the plug.

I stood in front of a nondescript office building far outside the city holding two paper cups filled with coffee - one black, one with cream and just a touch of sugar - while Henry dealt with the casting director inside. It was chilly and I had the bulky scarf my aunt knit me for Christmas wrapped tight around the bottom half of my face. I was trying to think of a way to drink the hot brown liquid without removing the comfort of the scarf when Henry appeared beside me. He beamed as he took back his cup.

"Ok, babe, the release forms are all sorted!" He bounced on the balls of his feet in excitement and looked out over the barren parking lot, "The casting director said someone will be here soon to drive us to location."

I nodded and looked longingly at my cup as I wondered why we couldn't wait inside the dingy office. Turning my head, I searched the windy road we had driven up only moments before. I was impatient to get the shoot started. The sooner we started, the sooner we'd finish. Henry had warned me it'd probably take all day and I was already regretting my decision to come. I strained my eyes trying to see further down the road, willing a vehicle to manifest. I held the cup of coffee in both my hands, the warmth penetrating the skin of my fingers and palms only slightly, the rest of my body shivering in the cold.

We only had to wait a few minutes before a grey windowless van pulled up in front of us. I eyed it suspiciously. Rust was beginning to eat away at the wheel wells and the grey paint was dull, having lost its luster long ago. I looked at Henry and silently begged him not to make me get into the van, but he wasn't looking at me. The driver's side door opened with a squeal and a young man jumped out.

He was slight and very chic-looking. His wool peacoat was fitted and the jeans and boots I could see beneath it were dark and fashionable. He wore round glasses and his beard was neatly trimmed close to his skin. A grey beanie was pulled over his ears and he smiled warmly at us as he brought a pen down to the clipboard in front of him.

"Henry Cooper and Claire Lane?"

"That's us!" Henry exclaimed. I waved unenthusiastically.

"Hi, I'm Brett. I'm the production assistant for today's shoot. The location is only a fifteen-minute drive from here." He slid the back door of the van open and Henry jumped in. I hesitated, looking from the worn cloth seat, yellow foam visible at the corners, to Brett.

Brett just smiled that warm professional smile at me. "I know it looks a little sketchy - they won't let us drive the prop vehicles, unfortunately."

I groaned beneath the thick wool yarn of my scarf and followed Henry. Brett slid the door shut behind me and I searched futilely for a seat belt. The van bounced and swayed as Brett hopped into the driver's seat. "Hope you guys like indie rock!" he called over his shoulder as the van rolled out of the parking lot and onto the main street.

The back of the van was surprisingly clean and I found myself becoming more comfortable with the situation. I could only see the road through the windshield but the winter sun shone through the bare trees and it felt nice to be so close to nature. Henry took my hand and gave it a gentle squeeze. I rested my head on his shoulder and smiled as a Modest Mouse song played over the van's speakers from Brett's iPod.

Twenty minutes later, we were both beginning to shift in our seats. My coffee cup rested empty in my hands and I had removed several layers as the car's dry heat started to make me sweat.

"Hey Brett, are we almost there?" Henry asked, peering around the passenger headrest in an attempt to see more of the road.

"Yep, any minute now!" He called back over his shoulders. The van jostled beneath me as he turned onto a dirt road stretching through the now dense trees.

"This is where we're filming?" I asked, looking around him. "We're in the middle of nowhere!"

Brett laughed goodnaturedly. "Yeah, easier to set up all our gear. You'll be surprised how much lighting and camera equipment we need for a minute-long commercial."

I lurched back into my seat as the van hit a pothole, my coffee cup falling to the ground. Bending down to retrieve it from under the seat, I touched something sharp. I hissed in pain and brought my finger to my lips instinctually. My tongue traced the source and the coppery taste of blood stung against my taste buds.

"The fuck?" I said under my breath as I bent my body down further so I could see. My coffee cup was rolling lazily with the sway of the vehicle, lightly bouncing off of a polished axe, the edge sharpened to a nasty point. My brow tightened in confusion.

"We're here!" Brett cried cheerily. I sat upright and peered around him. In front of us loomed a giant house, old and brittle looking like a haunted house leftover from Halloween. Windows were smashed in or boarded up and the wood walls were rotten and sagging under the weight of their age. Shutters, bricks, and glass littered the ground.

I looked at Henry with concern, but he only shrugged.

Brett pulled up in front of the house. He turned in his seat to face us, smiling, waiting for a reaction. I sat still, disbelieving the situation around me. Brett, unphased, grabbed his clipboard from the other seat and jumped out. Henry wouldn't make eye contact with me as the back door slid open. Brett stood there, his hand outstretched like a driver preparing to escort his fare out. I shook my head and scooted back into Henry.

Brett laughed and turned his head, "Bob, can I get some help with the talent?"

A beefy man covered in hair appeared in the door. "This is Bob, the gaffer," Brett explained as Bob reached towards me. I turned, pushing Henry to go deeper into the van. A strong hand wrapped around my ankle as I threw myself over the back of the seat. I kicked hard but struck only the winter air. Bob tugged and my hands slipped from the seat. Pain shot through my knee as I fell to the hard ground. Tears began to collect in my eyelashes.

Bob pulled on my leg, still in his grasp, and my chin hit the ground, more pain screaming through my body. My leg pulled at my hip socket as Bob started to drag me towards the house. I looked up to see Henry jump from the van and run towards me. Another big man, much taller than Bob, ran up to him and, using the bottom of his heavy work boot, kicked him in the side of the leg, right beneath his left knee. Henry fell with a sickening crack. He screamed in pain and I realized I was screaming as well. I clutched desperately at the dirt in front of me trying to stop Bob's progress. My fingernails tore upward as I tried to cling to the frozen earth moving beneath me.

The tall man picked Henry up and hoisted him over his shoulder like a bag of flour. Henry cried out and squirmed in his grasp. Bob stopped and my leg fell to the ground. I rolled over and saw that I was in front of a brand new SUV. Behind it, the trees stretched out towards the cold sun like forgotten bones.

"What the fuck?" My throat was hoarse, the tight and raspy sound of my voice foreign to me. My whole body shook and the tears that glazed my face were beginning to freeze.

Henry was dropped unceremoniously beside me and I grabbed him. We hugged each other, our bodies clinging together in desperate fear.

"Cameras ready?" The tall man yelled, his voice low and gravely, the words sounding as if they were rolling over jagged stones.

A small woman being swallowed by an oversized green army jacket held out a thumbs up from behind a giant camera. Brett ran up beside him, the clipboard in one hand, the axe I cut my finger on in the other. He looked towards us, that warm friendly smile from the office parking lot unmoving.

The sound of a throat clearing startled me and I looked back, ready for the next horror. Standing over us was an attractive man in a smart charcoal coat. He smiled down at me, his perfect teeth a bright white that contrasted sharply with the grey colors surrounding them.

"You guys ready?" He asked, his smooth voice viscous like oil, dripping from his lips.

"Wh-what?" I whimpered, "r-r-ready for what?"

"Places everyone." The tall man cried from beside the camera and the handsome man looked up towards him, smiling that dazzling smile.

"Camera rolling?"

"Rolling." The woman said.

"Ac-tion." The word was spoken meticulously, the man relishing every inch of it.

The handsome man looked down at us, "What do you guys think of the new Meridian?" He asked enthusiastically, gesturing to the car.

I looked at the car, then to the camera, then back to the handsome man with the white smile.

"Cut!" The tall man yelled. He bent down to pick something up. I screamed as he stood, a crowbar hanging loosely in his grip. He began to walk towards us, his heavy boots crunching the pine needles and leaves beneath him. I turned away, preparing to stand and run when I saw Bob watching me. His arms were crossed and a smile slowly formed on his thick lips. My knee twinged with pain.

No running. I thought. There won't be any running.

The tall man reached us and slowly knelt down so that he was eye to eye with us. He rested his weight on one knee and snarled, the crowbar resting on the ground beside him, his fingers lightly tracing its sides.

"Don't. Look. At. The camera." He growled. He stood stiffly, raised the crowbar, and swung it down onto my outstretched foot. The pain tore through my bone and muscle, electricity shooting through my body as I screamed in agony. The tall man walked back to the camera. I sobbed as I looked at my leg. Bone jutted out from torn flesh, as white as the handsome man's teeth. I tried to scream but the sound that emitted was pained and small, my voice no longer functioning. Henry hugged me closer, and I tried to swallow, to give my throat some relief, any relief, but my mouth was dry.

"Ready?" The tall man asked again. There was no answer. "Action!" He said, the word chopped short.

"Henry, Claire, what are your thoughts on the new 2018 Meridian?" The smooth voice asked from behind us.

I turned to look back at the man, who never stopped smiling at me. "W-why?" I choked, barely audible.

"What was that, Claire?" The man held his hand behind his ear, "I didn't catch that." He dropped his hand and gestured towards the SUV, "What are your thoughts on the new Meridian?"

"I… I…" My voice caught as more tears forced their way from my eyes. I couldn't speak without sobbing, so instead, I simply nodded, hoping to make the torture end.

The handsome man stepped around us, careful to avoid my injured foot, and walked towards the car.

"Well, what's a family SUV without family?" He pulled the back door open with a flourish.

My bloodcurdling scream filled the quiet winter air around me, piercing high into the sky. Four faces stared out from inside the car. I screamed again as their eyes widened in recognition. My mother, father, sister, and brother-in-law began to squirm and pull against the chains binding them to the seats. Their cries were muffled by dirty rags wrapped around their mouths. My niece, only five years old, was slumped over in one of the seats, completely unconscious. I tried to focus, to see if her chest was rising and falling, but I couldn't tell. Bruises and cuts lined their faces, their skin only clean of blood and dirt where rivers of tears had washed them away.

Before I knew it I was standing, all my weight on my good foot, my good knee. Bob's arms were wrapped around my waist as I struggled, flailing my arms wildly. I slapped and punched his solid mass, desperately trying to push myself forward while his meaty arms held me back.

The last thing I remember is something hard falling against the back of my head and the world going black.

I woke up in a hospital room yesterday with a mild concussion, a dislocated knee, and a shattered foot. They say I was found outside the doors of the emergency room early in the morning, bloodied and unconscious. I've repeated this story numerous times to the police, who are still searching for my family. I pray they are still alive.

The nurses are kind. One of them said she'd wash my clothes for me, but the police took them in as evidence. They were able to give me back my wallet though. All my cards and receipts were still there, even the Christmas check from my grandparents that I still hadn't cashed. As I looked through my wallet, the familiarity of it comforting me slightly, I noticed that one of the card pockets felt oddly thick. I pulled forward at my credit card and found a small, folded-up note behind it.

"I don't expect you to understand, but they promised me fame. I'm sorry and I hope you'll forgive me one day. I love you, babe."

The Bone Merchant

We barter with bones.

We save and scrimp. The delicate ivory sticks more valuable than money, gold, jewels. Because once a year, on Halloween, he comes to our small town.

The bone merchant.

He only accepts the bones of humans, ages fifteen to twenty, and not all bones will do. There does not seem to be a rhyme or reason to which bone is most highly valued. One year, it was a phalanx bone from the pointer finger. Another year only a rib would do. And so we collect the bones of the fallen.

The bone merchant has been coming for almost a decade and since his first appearance, the graveyard has been all but emptied. The graves of those of the desired age lay open and bare, a novel ripped from its pages. People's sons and daughters, their aunts and uncles, nieces and nephews and cousins, are nothing but symbolic plots of land. Nothing but dirt and a worn stone.

And so, people became desperate. It is not often one of the chosen ages reaches twenty-one. The nice folk in town have given up - they cannot afford the bone merchant's wares. The nicer of the others will buy hands and feet from desperate parents, knowing one day they will be worth all the riches in the world.

And then there are those who do not care about your family, or your happiness, or your life. Those that will kill a teenager on sight.

Mrs. Godor killed Mr. Hatchet's nephew in broad daylight. Despite all the Hatchets' locks and barred windows, they let her inside without question. She had been their neighbor for thirty years. Mr. Hatchet's kids were all grown, past the age of value long ago. Yet, the boy Mack, would not see those golden years.

She killed him in front of his extended family only to discover later that he was one month shy of his fifteenth year. She went to the gallows for nothing.

For the bone merchant can get you anything you could possibly want. From beauty, to health, to a lost love. The bone merchant sells what you cannot buy anywhere else.

My mother passed away a few months ago, and she left me her fortune: the bones of her dead brother. He died before I was born and was buried on our property, not in the town cemetery, so when the bone merchant began his yearly visits, she dug him up and hid him in the shed. She never used a bone, not even after my father died. She was saving it in case something horrible happened to me or my sister, but she was able to keep us safe till we turned twenty-one. I am twenty-eight now, my sister twenty-four, and I have my mother to thank for that.

No one knows about the bones in our shed, even my sister is unaware of just how rich we are.

But this year is my year. The year I finally get everything I want.

She's two years older than me and was safely twenty when the bone merchant first arrived. I've wanted her to be mine all of my life, but instead, she's lived her life without me as I hid myself and my sister from our neighbors and friends. She married Jacob, who sold his sister's bones for prosperity and fertility. They live in the large house on top of the hill, their four little girls free and safe for now.

Her name is Jocelyn and after this Halloween, she will be mine.

I smile as my fingers trace along the shin bone of my long-dead uncle, whom I never met.

If you had the power to buy anything, what would you buy?

The Miracle of Birth

TW: See Trigger Warning Appendix

It felt as if a knife had been stabbed deep into my abdomen, tearing through muscle as the tip touched the back of my insides. I screamed out as the pain brought me to my knees.

"We're going to the hospital," Noel said sternly, rubbing my back in an attempt to soothe me.

I had been experiencing sharp pains for weeks. At first, I dismissed them as particularly bad cramps. My period had been really light that month, more like spotting than an actual flow and I assumed the two had been related. It happened occasionally when I was on the pill so I initially wasn't worried. But the cramps continued long after my period had ended, gradually becoming worse and worse. Noel had been asking me to go to the doctor but I'd ignored him, brushing the pain off as normal.

My knees were barely propping me up from our kitchen floor as my body quaked in agony. In that moment even I had to agree that the pain had gone far past normal. I nodded to him, acknowledging that something was wrong. I stood, still shaking, and let my husband guide me out of the apartment.

"Congratulations Mrs. Gill, you're pregnant." The doctor smiled at me. I looked to Noel to see his response but his face was blank.

We were in our late twenties and financially stable, but while our Instagram feeds were filling up with pictures of nurseries and ultrasounds, we had both agreed that we weren't ready yet. Sure we talked about it, but it was always something for the future. We laughed and rolled our eyes when our mothers broached the subject, trying to gauge when we were going to start a family without asking outright. We told them that we were still having fun, that we still had time to enjoy our youth.

Yet, when I passed parents cooing at their newborns or playing with their toddlers, I would think about the joys of having kids. The love on their faces shone so pure and endless it made my heart pang with desire. But still, I wasn't ready.

The doctor's deep voice shook me from my thoughts, "How you proceed is your decision, but either way, we'll need to start scheduling your follow-up appointment as soon as possible."

My abdomen muscles tightened suddenly, so tight that it felt like a giant fist had balled itself inside my stomach and was threatening to punch its way out. I cried out as a burning pain spread throughout my lower stomach like molten lava. My body felt scorched as it flowed down towards my legs. I curled into the fetal position, hot tears beginning to form through my closed eyelids.

The doctor's voice was tight with worry as he continued, "These cramps you're experiencing are very concerning, especially since they've been occurring for so long. Please try to lie back so I can take a look."

I inhaled deeply, readying myself. As I exhaled I clenched my teeth and slowly unfurled my body. Whimpering from the pain, I placed my feet in the cold metal stirrups at the end of the exam table. The doctor bent down and placed his head between my thighs. I closed my eyes tight as a gloved hand cautiously pushed against the inside of my body. After a few seconds, there was a sensation of the hand leaving. I held my breath but the room remained silent. I opened my eyes hesitantly and was greeted by the doctor's grey gaze. His expression of alarm and disbelief made my stomach drop.

"We need to get you upstairs as soon as possible."

"Why, what's upstairs?" Noel asked, his voice thick with panic.

Never taking his eyes from mine the doctor answered. "The maternity ward."

"What? Why?" I demanded.

He swallowed, steadying himself. "Because you're 5 centimeters dilated. Whether you want a child or not, you're in active labor and we need to act now."

The world grew silent as shock washed over me. The past nine months flashed before my eyes: weekly sushi lunches, my morning cup of dark roast, the occasional cigarette, my regular after work beer, weekend shots of tequila, hell even my new tattoo. This child would most likely be deformed, mentally challenged, or dead. I shuddered. I could taste the acid of my bile as it burnt the back of my tongue.

I shook my head. No, it was impossible. How could I be pregnant? I had no symptoms and I sure as hell didn't look nine months pregnant. Despite my bad habits I had been trying to improve my health. I had been losing weight for weeks. I was on track to get back to my college weight by the end of the year.

I placed my hand on my lower stomach and felt nothing. I was empty. My hand stayed there as nurses passed me, the sounds of their shoes over the linoleum floor and the beeping of machines humming in my ears like a distant hurricane.

The frenzy was dying down when my doctor returned. He reached inside me and nodded to himself before sitting up. His voice was low and soothing, the tone one takes when speaking to a frightened child. "You're staying dilated at 5 centimeters so it seems like we have a little time. Let's take a look at what we've got here." A cold wet jelly was applied to my flat stomach, creating a slimy layer of goop. The doctor brought a grey ultrasound wand down onto my skin and began to drag it over my flesh. The steady hum of the room faded as a new sound floated up and surrounded us: a small steady heartbeat. I looked at the machine's black and white screen to see small washed-out shapes bob in and out of focus. It was pixelated and ill-defined, but I recognized it as a baby nonetheless. The baby I hadn't felt grow. The baby I hadn't helped, that I hadn't taken care of. The baby I hadn't even thought about or considered. Heavy tears rolled down my cheeks as I watched the baby, my baby, wiggle and squirm, its limbs barely moving within me.

I would've taken care of you, I thought. I would have taken care of you if I had known you were there.

As I listened to the heartbeat I thought of our tiny one-bedroom apartment filled with our bikes and paints and alcohol. All the toxic things we didn't consider as threats because they weren't. It was the home of adults without responsibilities. If we had known we could've prepared.

Could've found a bigger place, bought furniture, baby-proofed. We could've found a safe space for our tools and instruments and art supplies. Concern for my unborn child filled me. Regret soon followed. Regret that I wasn't able to prepare my life for a baby. That I wasn't able to bring it into a home that was ready for it. Parenthood had been far from my mind only a few hours ago, yet now I felt an attachment to the fully developed life inside me.

The doctor turned and smiled despite himself. "It's a boy."

Warmth flooded through me. Not the burning of pain but a good kind of warmth. A happy warmth. Love, I realized. It was love. I loved him.

An hour later I was screaming as pain exploded between my thighs. Through the blur of confusion and horror, I could hear the doctor telling me to breathe. My legs were wet and I could see fluid flowing from inside of me. I choked as a sob caught in my throat, threatening to suffocate me.

I knew nothing of childbirth. I tried to think back to educational films from middle school, but I was lost in pain, only able to do what I was told and pray that I was doing it right. With each wave of pain, I pushed as instructed, ignoring the primal fear screaming within me as my body tore itself apart. I could feel it, feel the child between my legs. I looked down and despite the dizzying red that painted my vision I could see a grey-blue ball emerge from my body. It was disgusting and beautiful at the same time.

Relief washed over me through the pain as I looked at his perfect face. He was ok. His features were scrunched with the agony of entering the world, but he was alive.

The doctor continued to pull and I felt my body loosen as my son's narrow shoulders appeared. A heat grew in my genitals and I cried out again with the effort as the doctor continued to pull, revealing my son's chest.

I looked down and screamed. It was a deep guttural scream. Not of pain, but of horror.

My baby boy's chest was skinless, his rib cage and organs completely exposed. The reds and purples of his insides deflated and spread apart from each other. As he became more and more exposed to the air of the hospital room his body melted, losing its structure.

"Oh, oh god!" The doctor exclaimed, his face twisted in disgust. Noel retched beside me. My body became numb as my infant's slippery legs fell from me leaving my body barren. His tiny heartbeat still resonated in my loins like a faraway echo.

No, no, no. He was alive. He had been alive. I had felt him. I had heard his heartbeat. A heartbeat that I had fallen in love within only a fleeting moment. A voice, my voice, rang throughout my head. Maybe he's still alive? Maybe they can save him?

I looked at his tiny heart, black and still. He wasn't coming back. I gasped for air in large, croaking inhales as I began to shake uncontrollably, pain and grief filling me until I could no longer take it and the world went dark.

Noel and I have never told anyone about what happened. It's too much to explain.

It's been three years and both of us still have nightmares about it. Nightmares of the pain and loss. I sometimes hear Noel crying in his sleep. He remembers the macabre horror, the fear. He remembers the half dissolved fetus falling apart in the doctor's hands.

But I also have dreams about our baby boy. Dreams of him surviving. Dreams of looking into his eyes and seeing the life within them. His tiny mouth opening to suck air into his new lungs before I awake suddenly, never able to stay and hear his first cry.

Planet X

Our solar system is a disc.

Remember those plastic 3D diagrams of our solar system from elementary school? The then-9 planets connected by thin metal wires to the large yellow sun in the middle? Well… yeah. That's what it looks like… in a way.

Our planet and several others orbit around our sun in this disc shape, but while the disk is mostly flat its edges lift upwards like a paper plate. A team from Caltech claims that this could be evidence of a massive planet at the edge of our system: Planet X. The reason we can't see Planet X is it's too far away for our modern telescopes to register. The light from our sun has to travel all the way past Neptune, past the Kuiper Belt, bounce off of Planet X, and come all the way back, the light fading exponentially with every stage of its journey.

At least that's what they hypothesize.

But I know the truth. Planet X doesn't want us to see them.

The dreams started a year ago. I would fall asleep only to immediately wake up somewhere else. Initially, I thought of it as an alien zoo, like the one described in Kurt Vonnegut's Slaughterhouse-Five. That first night is still vivid in my memory.

I awoke in a small white room, bare except for a large spherical object. It was as large as a dining room table and even had a flat top, its sides white and smooth just like the walls.

As I stood, I realized I was standing in water. I looked around and saw that I was in a shallow pool lined with small black stones which were cool and smooth to the touch. Before me was a wall made of glass. I stepped to it, pressing my face against it as I looked out towards a lush nightscape. Despite the darkness, the campus around me was illuminated by green and purple vegetation that glowed in the dim light. Large blooms the size of my entire body, ranging in colors from dull pink to bright yellow, loomed over my room like jungle trees, the bioluminescent lights within them shining like tiny stars in the night. Twisted vines extended from the organic roof to the ground, which was made up of a coarse reddish dirt.

I immediately noticed that my room was not unique. Across from me rose a wall of similar squares filled with beings of all shapes and sizes, many of which my mind couldn't even fathom.

In one room was a perfect triangle of pure white light. I was surprised to find that it wasn't too bright or hot to look at and I stared at the light for several minutes, mesmerized. Soon my head began to buzz with a combination headache and brain freeze. It felt as if there was a needle drilling into my skull through my eye. I ripped my gaze from the creature and the sensation vanished. I avoided looking at that room again.

The room above that one held a being like our werewolf. It was bipedal and shaped like a human man, but covered in a dense coarse fur, a mix of black and silver. Its hands ended in long claws with black webbing between bones shaped like fingers. Its teeth were large and sharp like a wolf's, yet instead of proportional dog ears, its ears were huge and conical. The beast also lacked any eyes from what I could tell. I assumed it was able to read space from echolocation like a bat, yet I never actually saw it move. It simply sat on the floor of its cage and looked out the window it didn't seem to see.

Above the werewolf-bat was a giant millipede. It looked and moved exactly like an earth millipede but was thicker than a grown man and longer than a limousine. The room was too small for it to stretch out so it coiled on top of itself, its many legs moving together like an ocean wave.

The most interesting of the rooms appeared to be completely empty. Yet, if you looked at it from your peripheral, the air in the room began to wave like heat rising from black tarmac. I felt a warmness when I looked into this room. A subtle bliss, as if I were drunk but it wasn't anything like being drunk. It was a wave of warmth through my body that made my skin prickle with satisfaction at an unknown, unrecognized touch.

Across from me was an alien much like a human woman. Her body was that of our world: two legs, two arms, two breasts, two eyes, a nose in the center of her face and hair on the top of her head. From a distance, I would've thought she was human but I was close enough to see the subtle differences. The skin of her stomach was interrupted by five small circles that looked like belly buttons. Her eyes were an unnatural yellow -- more like gold foil than an earth eye color. The long brown hair that hung over her shoulders swayed as if in a breeze, yet if her room was as identical to mine as it seemed, there wouldn't be any air to move it. She caught my gaze and smiled, nodding in my direction.

I woke up in a cold sweat. My arms shook with the effort of lifting myself from my bed. It was several hours before I needed to get up for work, but I knew I wouldn't be getting back to sleep. I took a shower, the hot water drumming into my skin, renewing the circulation of my blood and revitalizing my muscles which felt atrophied.

Work was the usual boring humdrum. I couldn't focus, the dream from the night before echoing in my mind. Ever since I left the warmth of my shower my skin felt cold and clammy. My boss even commented on my sweater.

"You know it's June, right George?" She chuckled.

I smiled good-naturedly as I struggled to control my shivering.

That night, I dreamt of the zoo again. The woman smiled at me. I waved to her. She looked confused at first before returning the gesture, which appeared awkward and unnatural to her. I smiled.

This repeated for months. Every night I would dream of waking in the zoo. It felt so real, so tangible. I could feel the material of the walls, similar to plastic but spongier. With every dream, the woman and I would communicate more. First through simple gestures, like waving and nodding, then progressing to more complicated thoughts.

Her hands hovered over her eyes before she brought them down quickly. She was sad.

I touched the glass between us, then pointed at her and then to myself. I wanted to meet her.

She touched the glass, then knocked on it, then shook her head. We would never meet.

I gestured sad and she nodded.

I pointed to myself and then to her and then to my heart. I hugged myself. Friend.

She hugged herself in return. It was amazing how similar our alien minds worked. How universal some thoughts and feelings really seemed to be.

The zoo was a strange place, neither bad nor good. I never saw any spectators or even anyone who seemed in charge of the zoo. We were never fed or taken care of. We just were.

The woman and I grew closer with every dream. It was as if she were real. The bond I felt with her was so deep, it couldn't all be a figment of my imagination.

We couldn't tell each other our names, so I thought of her as Remi. Remi was the name of my younger brother, Derek's stuffed lion as a kid. Derek passed away a few years ago. He had been born deaf and mute and I think he would've liked Remi.

Every time I woke up in the zoo I would go to the window. Remi would greet me every time by signing sad before hugging herself. She was sad but my friendship helped.

I asked Remi how long she had been there.

A long time, she said. She gestured to the sky and brought her hands from her eyes downward. She missed home.

I gestured to the sky and pointed to myself, closing my eyes as if I were asleep, and pointed back to the sky. I go home in my sleep.

Remi repeated my gestures and then aggressively shook her head.

I brought my hand to my chin, our sign for a question. I didn't understand.

Remi repeated the gestures, pointed to herself, and then shook her head.

I pointed to her, then to the sky, made the motion for sleep, and then shook my head.

She nodded. She used to go home in her sleep.

I brought my hand to my chin. What happened?

Remi opened her mouth in a scream, her face twisted in anger. I heard nothing, the sound trapped within her walls. Suddenly she turned wild, jumping and stomping, her hair spinning around her head, whipping back and forth as if caught in a hurricane. Her body twisted, suddenly boneless, a slug being pulled at either end. Finally, she stopped and looked at me, her hair calming enough to rest mostly still by her face, now streaked with black tears. She pointed to the white sphere in her room and then to the sky. I followed her finger, my heart pounding in my chest. Fear gripped at me tightly. I had never seen Remi look or act like this. She was no longer sad, she was angry.

Turning away from me, she walked to the white sphere in her room and touched the top. She looked up expectantly. I walked to the matching object in my room and placed my hand on it. Nothing happened. I looked up and she raised her hand in the air to make a circular gesture. Using my fingertip, I made a circle on the flat surface.

74

I jumped with surprise as the top of the object lit up with a blue light. It was a computer screen. In the middle was a circle as small as a marble that I recognized as earth from a great distance.

Remi pointed to the sky. Looking up through the alien canopy I could see a faint yellow star, closer than any other star yet still barely larger than a pinprick.

She pointed to me. The sun. Our sun.

I jolted upright, my bedroom unfamiliar around me in the twilight.

The next night I opened my eyes to the now-familiar ceiling. I went to sit but I was unable to move. Struggling, I realized with immediate panic that I was restrained. I looked as far to the right as possible, straining my eyes to see something, anything. My head was being held in place but I was able to make out the black stones beneath me which glowed like the bioluminescent plants outside. I looked back up and screamed as my vision was filled by a new alien creature hovering inches above my face.

Its skin looked like a seal's, soft and wet. The head that hung over me was featureless except for hundreds of glowing black shapes, identical to the stones I laid on. Around its head was a thick mane of what looked like a mix of seaweed and fur. One of the appendages around its neck stretched towards me and I futilely tried to squirm from its reach. As its flesh touched mine white-hot heat sizzled against my skin. It felt like I was being branded by the sun. My screams were no longer able to produce any sound, the only escape for my fear and pain abruptly cut off.

More heat began to crawl from its touch like veins reaching across my skin. As the sensation hit my chest I felt it inch towards my heart, which convulsed erratically under the heat's weight. My throat began to burn as it rose inside of me, filling my entire being. It was as if I were being squeezed from the inside out.

And then I woke up, my bed once again soaked. My stomach ached from the pain of my dream and I lightly brushed my fingers over the area. A pained hiss escaped through my clenched teeth and I tentatively lifted my shirt. Beneath my ribs was a large circular burn that puckered and oozed. My breath caught in my chest, a sensation I hadn't felt since I fell off my bike as a child, my back slamming into the hard concrete. I gasped like a fish as my throat struggled to claim the air my lungs needed. My face was wet with tears.

I called out of work that day. And the next. Every night I woke to that, that thing. Every night it touched me in a different spot and every night I was filled with a different pain. Sometimes it was the burning of the first night.

Sometimes it forced its way through me like ice, slow and solid, the freezing pain seizing in my muscles, my heart straining to beat. Once it was sharp and stabbing, as if my flowing blood had turned into hundreds of needles.

Every morning I woke, my body bruised and battered. I was cut, burnt, bloodied, and torn. My veins grew dark beneath my skin like black trails etched into the fabric of my being.

I tried to go to the doctor but they dismissed me as a junkie. The frequent calls out of the office lost me my job. Eviction notices started to pile up inside my door. But none of that matters.

Last night was the first night in weeks I awoke unrestrained. Crying with relief, I stood, my legs shaking beneath me. The first thing I noticed was that, for the first time, it was day. I blinked, my eyes unused to the light as I looked to Remi, who stood with her hand against the glass. A gesture I was happy to reciprocate.

The forest around me glowed in the radiance of the light. As my eyes began to adjust, I was overwhelmed by the surprisingly bright and vibrant colors of the forest around me. I beamed at Remi. It was beautiful but Remi's face was drawn tight in concern. She pointed to me, then to herself, then to the stone pool behind her. She shook violently, her face clenched as if in pain. They had tortured her too.

I brought my hand to my chin. Why?

She pointed up.

There in the sky, a fire burned. Not like a sun, but a much smaller and closer glowing sphere of heat. A stream of fire stretched like a tail from the ball as it flew over us, a caricature of a comet. It wasn't day, instead, the world was illuminated by a massive rocket more than fifty times the size of any I had seen on TV.

I looked back at Remi who pointed to herself, then to me. Sad. She pointed to the screen beside me. I stepped to it and made the circular motion to turn it on. The small marble earth appeared, as it always did. I tilted my head. Something was off. I leaned closer to get a better look. In the foreground of the screen there was nothing but blackness where usually there was a cluster of stars. A part of space was empty where it shouldn't be.

I looked to Remi. Sad.

I pointed to the screen and brought my hand to my chin. What is it?

Remi pointed to the rocket, then to my screen, and then back to the sky. They were coming.

I shook my head as I stepped back from the screen in shock. No.

Yes. Sad.

No.

Yes. Sleep. Home. Sad.

No.

I brought my hands together and pulled them apart as far as I could. Far. Too far. Earth was too far.

Remi closed her eyes as if in sleep, then opened them, closed them, opened them, faster and faster. Time. She closed her eyes one final time, keeping them closed before slowly opening them and looking at me. Time passing. She pointed to the pool behind her, then to me.

I looked back to the sky. The rocket, a giant ball of fire and metal, hung heavy above the atmosphere. I shook my head and looked back to Remi. Far, I gestured again. Even with their advanced technology, it would take Planet X more than a millennium to travel to earth.

She pointed to the pool and then to me and repeated the gesture for time passing. I shook my head and brought my hand to my chin. I don't understand.

Remi pointed to the ground, the zoo, then to herself, then to the sky, to the screen in my room, and then to the pool. Time passing. Here. Remi. The pool. Time passing. Earth. Here. Remi. Time passing. Earth. The pool. She pointed to the screen. Information. She pointed to me. Information. Time passing. Earth. Me. The pool. Information.

Time passing. It would take millennia for the aliens to reach earth. Time passing. The pool I always woke up in. Time passing. My head spun.

She pointed to herself and her screen, then to the sky. Remi. Remi's home. Time passing. And then she screamed, her mouth stretching as it had only one time before when I had asked why she was sad. She stopped and looked at me.

I shook my head, stepping backwards. No. No. No no no no.

Remi pointed at me and then brought her hands to her eyes. Sad.

My stomach dropped and my mind buzzed. I looked up at the rocket which appeared to hover above us, then back to the screen which showed the same rocket approaching earth.

I wasn't being brought across space. I was being brought across time as well.

I looked to Remi, who nodded. Why?

Remi pointed to the screen. Information. They wanted to know what we'd be like when they got there.

I fell to my knees. No. It couldn't be. I looked up. Remi was waving.

Sad. Goodbye.

I woke up.

You Don't Know What You've Got Till It's Gone

Would you describe yourself as spoiled?

My pencil glided over the paper, a smooth trail of graphite following. With a satisfying scratch, I circled "No." The smell of fresh paper and pencil shavings took me back to high school. Before I was an adult. Before I knew how difficult life could get.

Would you describe your close friends as spoiled?

I hesitated.

First, there was Meredith. Meredith, whose parents made damn sure she never endured hardship. Who paid for her Ivy League degree out of pocket and financed extended trips abroad in the name of their only child's self-discovery. Who owned the luxury apartment Meredith called her own. Who nested her in the comfort of unearned extravagance.

Meredith is an artist, they'd say. Meredith is a tortured soul who needs freedom to work on her novel without the hideous distraction of a 9 to 5. She is a creative who cannot be caged by the struggle of the common folk but must sit and be and think and ponder and write and give a voice to the common folk and their struggle.

Then there was Erica. Erica, who glided by on her looks. Who didn't have to work on her personality because she didn't need one. Who could be rude without consequence. Her instincts unchecked, her id free to roam. Why would she think about you when everyone won't stop thinking about her? It's not inconsiderate if there's nothing to consider. If she forgot who you were, you should've made yourself more memorable.

I circled "Yes."

My eyes scanned the last question.

On a scale of 1-10 with 1 being the least, how appreciative are you of what you have?

What did I have? A shitty job, a tiny overpriced apartment. Jiggly upper arms, frizzy hair. My hand hovered over the 4. Robert's warm smile. His soft kisses.

Sighing, I circled 8. I had shelter, a stable relationship, and a loving family. Life was good, even if other people had it better than me.

Around me were 11 other people seated at small identical desks completing short identical surveys. Different shapes and sizes, ages and races. All completely forgettable.

A woman in her mid-twenties sat at the front of the room poking at a tablet. She wore a neat expensive-looking grey sweater. Her brown hair was pulled back into a tight bun. The desk she sat at was modern but simple, the desktop empty but for a plain water bottle. Both the desk and woman looked like they were from an IKEA catalog. Generic but tidy, desirable but empty.

I walked towards her, my completed survey in hand. She looked up from her tablet with a small smile and gestured to the corner of the desk.

Her voice was smooth but neutral, "thank you, Laurie."

I placed my answers face down beside her, completing the nostalgic experience of taking a quiz.

"Please proceed to the waiting room. We will get you once it has been processed."

Not wanting to make additional noise, I nodded and silently smiled at her but she was already looking back at her screen.

An hour later I sat in front of another tasteful but bland desk. Dr. Howden scanned the tablet in front of him, his fingertips pressed together.

Finally, he looked up at me. "Thank you for participating in our study, Ms. Cartland. We here at the Galvin Institute depend on volunteers such as yourself."

Three hundred dollars to come fill out a survey, yeah no problem mister. "Of course," I said politely.

"We'd like to invite you to continue as a participant. The study is six days and pays nine hundred dollars a day, along with a thousand-dollar completion bonus after your final day."

My mouth fell open. "Sorry, how much?"

Dr. Howden's smile tightened. "At the completion of the study, you will have been awarded six thousand and four hundred dollars."

I quickly calculated the cost of my morals. Is it worth six thousand and four hundred dollars to inject myself with something that would make me lose all my hair? I shrugged internally. It'll grow back. Probably. There's always wigs.

"Is the study risky?"

"Oh no, not at all. All we ask of you is to answer 3 simple questions every day."

"You just want me to answer questions?"

Dr. Howden opened one of the desk drawers and placed a tablet in front of me. It was identical to both his and the woman from the survey room.

"The Galvin Institute will provide you with this tablet for the duration of the study. Every night at 6 pm it will notify you to answer three simple questions. You will then have an hour to answer them. Once your answers are submitted, nine hundred dollars will be directly deposited into your bank account." He looked at me over his wire frames. "Do you accept?"

My heart thudded in my chest. "What happens if I answer incorrectly?"

He smiled again. "The questions are subjective, so there is no wrong answer."

I bit my lip, looking down at the desktop in front of me. There must be a catch. There's always a catch. Hesitant to accept his insane offer without some sort of probing, I looked back up. "Can I opt-out at any time?"

His smile faltered for a moment before he continued. "Of course, but you will forfeit all payment up to that point."

I picked up the tablet and examined it. On the back was a subtle green logo with the initials "GI" in a pyramid.

Dr. Howden continued. "The focus of this study is appreciation and gratitude. The questions are designed to encourage self-reflection."

I nodded. "Sounds easy."

"It is!" he said, turning his own tablet towards me to reveal an electronic contract. He held out a thin stylus. "Oh, and please note that your tablet is programmed to only ask the questions and cannot be used for any other purpose."

The drag of the stylus was smooth and frictionless as I signed my name.

"Thank you, Ms. Cartland. We look forward to working with you here at the Galvin Institute."

"This has to be a scam," Robert said, his beer hovering in front of his mouth as he eyed the tablet resting on the table beside us. We had both tried playing with it but the screen would only illuminate to show a timer counting down to six pm. No games, no other screens.

I shrugged. "The building was super nice and it all seemed on the up and up. I doubt they're going to try and use my information to drain my bank account or something. Besides," I rested my hand on his, "it's for the wedding."

He sighed. "You know, you've got to stop pushing that."

I stuck my tongue out at him teasingly.

A loud electric jingle made me jump. The screen of the tablet was now bright white. Black font was neatly written across at the top.

I picked it up as Robert stood to look over my shoulder. On the screen was a question:

What was something bad that happened to you today?

Other than applying for the study my day had been pretty uneventful. I clicked my tongue thoughtfully before answering.

Nothing.

A circle appeared at the bottom right corner that read "submit." I pressed it and the second question appeared:

What was something good that happened to you today?

I smiled.

Dinner with my boyfriend.

Robert kissed my head as I hit submit.

On a scale of 1-10, with 1 being the least, how appreciative are you of what you have?

The numbers one through ten were beneath in small circles. I felt Robert's warmth beside me and pressed "9."

The tablet made a small chime as the words "Thank you!" jumped on screen. Little bits of blue and yellow confetti fell around it before the screen went black again.

My blood vibrated hot beneath my skin as I excitedly logged into my bank's mobile app. My checking account was, indeed, nine hundred dollars larger.

"Not a bad day's work," Robert said as he returned to his seat.

I woke up the next morning to the shrill sound of my phone ringing. I looked at the clock. Seven thirty-one am.

"Come on!" I groaned at the ceiling. I closed my eyes tightly before opening them again, my room slowly focusing around me. Without looking I reached over and yanked it from its charger. My phone's screen was filled with the smiling face of Meredith. I groaned again as I answered.

"Dude, it's Saturday. What--." A high-pitched squeal interrupted me.

"Random House bought my book!!!"

I sat bolt upright. "Sorry, what?"

"Random House, Laurie. Fucking Random House!!"

The meaning of her words slowly dawned on me through the cloud of sleep.

"Random House -- the publisher -- bought your book?" I asked, incredulous.

"Yes!! Ah, we need to get coffee NOW!"

Thirty minutes later I sipped my latte while Meredith regaled me with the story.

"I thought it was really weird when they scheduled a meeting super early on a Saturday morning, but it's Random House, so I couldn't say no! Apparently one of their agents saw some of the chapters I published online and fell in love!! They're offering me a seventy-five thousand dollar advance!"

I choked on the warm liquid running down my throat.

"I know, right!?" Meredith squealed.

"Seventy-five grand!?" The words came from my mouth violently as I tried to regain control of my breath. "Seventy-five grand for your first novel!?"

Meredith nodded, beaming.

"It's not even done!"

"Oh, I know! I know! But you know what, I think this is really going to help motivate me to finish! My skin is tingling with creative juices!"

Your skin is tingling with seventy-five grand. I bit back my tongue and gave her a weak smile.

"Congratulations Meredith. That's awesome."

Meredith and I had met in college. We were both wannabe novelists, both women, both freshmen, and both living in the same dorm. We didn't become friends because we connected artistically, we became friends because it was easy.

While I had thrived in school, Meredith had coasted. She graduated because she went to most of her classes and turned in most of her homework. Like our friendship, she succeeded because she didn't fail.

After graduation, I got a job in publishing as an editorial assistant. I was paid the bare minimum to review encyclopedias written by retired middle school teachers. It sucked but it was a job. Without it, I'd be homeless.

Meredith was a trust fund kid. I was not.

I made a point of working on my novel for at least three hours every week. I was sixty thousand words deep into a dramatic look at the repression of women in the early 19th century through the eyes of Charlotte, a lowly chambermaid working for a handsome but distant oil tycoon. Meredith, on the other hand, would write a few pages when the mood struck. Since graduating, we met monthly to discuss our progress and keep each other motivated, but more often than not the night would devolve into expensive drinks at bars filled with men with shirts inexplicably half unbuttoned. And while I woke up regretting all my decisions and trying not to vomit in my cubicle trash can, she'd remain untouched. She'd wake up at noon to order pizza and watch a marathon of shitty reality shows about overly dramatic rich people who also didn't have any responsibilities.

Meredith's novel, smartly titled A Rabbit Disturbed, was about an evil toy bunny that traumatizes a young boy. Imagine if Stephenie Meyer wrote a novel adaptation of The Velveteen Rabbit after watching the entire Chucky canon while on acid. Oh, and also Miss Meyer inexplicably doesn't seem to know what a rabbit is.

The three chapters I've read, the only three Meredith has bothered to write, were so bad that my main criticism was towards our college for giving her a degree in creative writing.

But maybe I was being pretentious. Maybe I just didn't understand Meredith's genius. I took another swallow of my latte as she planned out the evening's celebratory activities as if planning a bachelorette party.

I was in a bar bathroom when the tablet chimed. I steadied myself against the sink before pulling it from my bag.

What was something bad that happened to you today?

It was early but my mind was already drenched in vodka. I definitely wasn't happy. I had thought drinking would make me feel more euphoric, would let me get caught up in Meredith's excitement, but instead I felt ineffectual and ignored. I thought of my novel and the stupid melodramatic character that I had poured all my creativity into for the past two years. I was miserable. Frustrated and defeated.

But what was I going to write? That one of my oldest friends had succeeded?

If you have nothing nice to say, say nothing at all. With my bare fingertip, I rubbed my answer against the screen.

Nothing.

What was something good that happened to you today?

I gritted my teeth.

Nothing.

On a scale of 1-10, with 1 being the least, how appreciative are you of what you have?

I pressed "3" without much thought and dropped the tablet back into my bag as the bright "Thank you!" lit up the screen.

I woke up Sunday with a pounding headache. I looked at my phone to see several Facebook and Instagram notifications. All likes and comments on the many celebratory photos I was tagged in, all congratulating Meredith. I let my phone fall from my hand as I turned over, allowing myself to sleep in.

The chime of the Galvin Institute tablet rang out as I sat on my couch mindlessly watching tv.

What was something bad that happened to you today?

It was an innocent question. At least, it seemed innocent. And yet I felt a pang of frustration. Meredith was still riding the high of the best day of her life while I sat there very consciously not working on my novel. Robert was busy with his family all night, leaving me alone to wallow in my self-pity.

I wrote "hangover" before clicking submit.

What was something good that happened to you today?

I lifted the stylus, preparing to write "nothing," but stopped short. This was a study of gratitude and here I was with absolutely none. I thought of Dr. Howden reading my responses. Judging them.

I got to sleep in.

On a scale of 1-10, with 1 being the least, how appreciative are you of what you have?

I pushed thoughts of Meredith out of my head as I surveyed my apartment. It was small and sparsely furnished, but the walls were lined with well-read novels. I hugged my soft throw and took a sip of my tea, letting the warmth flood down into my stomach. Ignoring the split second of burning at the back of my throat that told me it was still too hot to drink that fast. Feeling as if I had thoroughly experienced a moment of mindful appreciation, I pressed the tip of the stylus against the seven with a sense of accomplishment. I was rising above my disappointment and struggle.

Dr. Howden would be proud.

My phone vibrated and I was surprised to see a text message from Robert's mother.

Hi Laurie! Happy early birthday! Are you and Robbie free next weekend to come over for a birthday dinner?

My eyebrows scrunched together in confusion. That's odd. Why wouldn't she just ask Robert since he's there? Did he already leave?

Curious, I called him. He answered on the fourth ring.

"Hey, what's up?"

"Oh hey, is this a good time?"

"Sorry love, I'm still with my parents. Can I call you back afterwards?"

Icy fingers clasped around my heart. I swallowed.

"Oh, sure. Um, do you want to come spend the night when you're done? I miss you."

There was a pause before he continued. "Sorry, Laurie. I can't tonight. Maybe tomorrow."

"Okay. I love you."

"Love you too."

The next morning I lay in bed feeling empty, worthless, and defeated.

I stared at my ceiling, trying to rationalize staying in the comfort and safety of my bed. What would happen if I just didn't go to work? I'm so unimportant. Would anyone even notice?

It was bagel Monday though, and I did like bagels.

Three hours later I sat at my desk regretting my decision. One of the other editorial assistants had called out sick and I was getting the brunt of my boss' post-weekend wrath.

How fucking ironic, I thought as I scrolled past unread email after unread email. One email was three paragraphs of all caps red text berating me for the misspelling of Juan Ponce de León in an entry that was written and published five years before I was hired. I took a bite of my free bagel as I kept scrolling.

At lunch, Erica and I went to our favorite burger joint. Erica was an editor and close friend whose green almond eyes and vivacious figure made her the center of attention more often than not, and she knew it. She could be narcissistic at times, but she could also be really sweet and what I needed that day were fried food and a friendly ear.

Her eyes lit up and she leaned in conspiratorially. "Maybe he's ring shopping," she whispered, raising a perfectly manicured eyebrow.

I brought a french fry to my lips. I hadn't thought of that. I put the fry back down on the plate untouched.

"You really think so?" I asked, butterflies fluttering low in my stomach.

She winked before taking a bite of her burger.

Returning to my cubicle, my high spirits were immediately dashed by an unread email marked important. The subject line was empty and only two words were written, all lowercase, in the body of the email: see me.

Harold Bradford sat behind his desk, the glow of his computer illuminating his glasses. He was a chubby man in his late fifties with wiry grey hair that wrapped around his head leaving a round dome of perfectly hairless scalp in the middle. It shone in the fluorescent lights of his office like the golden dome of a synagogue.

"You wanted to see me, sir?"

"Yes, please sit down Ms. Cartland." He said, his eyes never leaving the screen. "This will only take a minute."

I sat down as he continued to tap at his keyboard. I pulled the hem of my skirt mindlessly as my eyes scanned the shelves of books behind him.

Finally, he looked up.

"Ms. Cartland, I asked you here to discuss your recent work performance."

My stomach sank.

"Your work has been…" he tilted his head back, eyeing me through his thin spectacles, "slipping."

A heavy silence fell between us.

"I-I-I'm sorry, Mr. Bradford," I stammered.

"You seem to think this job is… beneath you." He sniffed. "And while your BFA from Columbia is quite impressive, your work here lately is not."

"I understand." I nodded, cringing at the waiver in my voice. "I promise to work harder in the future."

"There is no future, Ms. Cartland."

I stared at him, mouth agape.

He turned back towards his computer, "Mrs. Littleton will explain your severance package."

My body and mind were numb as I left his office.

The warm water lapped at my skin as I sat in the bathtub. A glass of white wine stood at the side of the tub, the half-empty bottle on the floor. Robert had suggested that I could use this time to work on my novel, but I knew that was misguided. I needed to immediately focus all my attention on finding a job. Once that severance ran out, I wouldn't be able to pay my rent, let alone my bills or student loans. Oh sure, there's forbearance but that's just an ugly band-aid. The interest would gather like bacteria in an infection, following me for the rest of my life.

The smell of Robert's spaghetti and meatballs permeated the steam of the bathroom and I felt slightly comforted.

What was something bad that happened to you today?

I was fired.

What was something good that happened to you today?

I brought the stylus down, thinking I'd write something like, "my soon-to-be fiance was there for me," but I hesitated. I thought of the phone call last night. The uneasy feeling that came with it.

Instead, I wrote, "Bagel Monday."

On a scale of 1-10, with 1 being the least, how appreciative are you of what you have?

"Babe!"

The sound shook me and I jumped, cold water splashing around me.

"Babe, wake up!" I squinted to see Robert looking down at me.

"What happened?" I sat up and looked around. The wine glass had fallen from the tub, shattering on the tile floor.

"It's okay, stay there."

He left and I stood, grabbing my towel from the door and wrapping it around my shivering body. I must've been dreaming.

"What time is it?" I asked the empty room.

"Almost seven. You've been in there for almost two hours."

Panic rose like an electric shot through my spine.

"The tablet! Where's the tablet!" I cried, jumping out of the bath. Glass cut into the bottom of my foot. "Ow, fuck!" I cried.

Robert appeared in the doorway holding a broom. "Laurie, stop! What are you doing?"

"The survey! The survey!" I pushed him out of the way, limping into the living room. "Where is it? Where's my bag?"

Robert grabbed my arm. "Laurie you're injured, stop!"

"Nine hundred dollars!" I desperately pulled myself from his grasp, falling painfully to my knees. "Nine hundred dollars!"

The alarm rang distantly from where my bag lay forgotten by the front door. I crawled towards it, shaking with sobs. I could hear Robert talking to me as I reached it but his words were muffled and inconsequential. As I opened my bag my hands felt bloated and numb as if I were wearing gloves. My fingers clasped around the hard familiar plastic and I pulled the tablet out.

4 seconds remained on the timer. Tears flooded my eyes as I poked desperately at the screen but it wouldn't respond to my waterlogged touch.

"No, no, no." The black digits counted down to 1 before dissolved into nothing.

A wave of despair crashed over me as I watched the numbers appear once again. 23:59:03. The seconds ticked down. Tiny insults adding to the bloody mess of my ego.

The next thing I remember was waking up late in the afternoon. My body was sore, my head foggy. A sharp pain radiated from my left foot and I wanted to cry but there were no more tears.

There was a buzzing coming from my nightstand. I picked up my phone to see a new text message alert.

Hey babe

I stared at the words in confusion. Behind me, I could hear the shower running. Robert hadn't left. I saw the name at the top of the screen. "Erica."

That's odd. I opened the app to a chat I didn't recognize. Messages I didn't remember sending or receiving. I scrolled up to an image. It was a selfie of Erica. She was wearing lingerie.

Realization hit like a cement brick. The phone in my hand wasn't mine.

The shower stopped. My breaths grew short and ragged, catching in my throat in sharp gasps.

"Babe, are you okay?"

A shadow filled the door and approached me as my vision turned red.

I awoke on a hard, cold surface. I tried to move but my body screamed in pain. A bright light hurt my eyes as I slowly blinked them open. The room was grey and dingy. I sat up stiffly and looked in front of me at a wall of metal bars.

My head buzzed with questions, my eyes wide and seeing, no longer blinded or discomforted by the sudden light. I was sitting on a dirty tiled floor, a tall figure standing before me on the other side of the bars. It was a policewoman.

"Glad to see you finally awake, Ms. Cartland."

"Wh-what happened? Where am I?" I tried to recall recent memories. The bath. My foot. Erica. Robert.

"We got a call about a domestic disturbance at your residence. You were found standing over your boyfriend's body, a pair of bloody scissors..."

The cop continued but the sound was eclipsed by a sharp ringing noise in my head. My brain buzzed with shock as I sat back against a wall, bringing my knees to my chest. The room began to spin and it felt like I was falling into the buzzing. Into the void of complete and utter surrender.

An electronic alarm echoed off the cement walls. It was shrill enough and oddly familiar enough, to burrow into my numb thoughts.

"It's six o'clock, Ms. Cartland."

I looked up to see the cop holding out the Galvin Institute's tablet through the bars of the cell. I stared at it, uncomprehending.

"It's time to take the survey."

"What?" I looked at the cop, tears forming at the corners of my eyes.

The cop cleared her throat and dropped her arm, the tablet hanging uselessly beside her.

"What was something bad that happened to you today?"

I looked at her with confusion and pain.

"What was something good that happened to you today?" The cop's voice was flat and stiff. Robotic.

A sob broke out of my mouth violently. I clutched my hands to my ears, desperately trying to block out her voice.

"On a scale of 1-10, with 1 being the least, how appreciative are you of what you have?"

I opened my mouth, a scream pouring from my throat like vomit, filling the small room.

Reality snapped around me as if a door opened in a vacuum. The world sucked past my body as I ascended painfully to the heavens.

My eyes were assaulted once again with a bright light, but this light was softer. Cleaner. Nicer. I was in a white room, a simple desk in front of me. Behind it sat Dr. Howden.

"Thank you, Ms. Cartland, for your participation in the study." The corners of his eyes wrinkled with a warm smile.

My breaths came to me in gasps. I looked around at the innocuous room. It was just like it had been days before.

"I... I don't understand."

Dr. Howden gave me a tight smile. "Only a few hours have passed since you completed your initial intake survey. You have been under electronic hypnosis. Since signing the contract none of your actions, or the actions of your loved ones, actually occurred. It was all..." he tapped his temple, "in your head. I gave you a slight sedative before you awoke to help the transition along. You should be feeling more…" he smiled, "relaxed soon."

I nodded dumbly. The numbness weighing my body down was no longer raw and uncomfortable but calming.

"Now," he said, sliding a tablet across the desk, "if you'd please sign these release forms, you can be on your way."

Unable to process everything, I mindlessly brought my hand up. It shook slightly as I reached out and drew a simple line across the center of the page.

"Very good. You may now be excused. Your designated contact is waiting in the lobby."

I stood uncertainly and began to leave the room before he added, "Oh, and as I explained before, since you opted out prematurely you forfeit all reimbursement."

My stomach tightened as I saw Robert. His face set in bored concentration as he scrolled through his phone. Feeling my stare, he looked up and smiled warmly. "Hey!" He stood and walked towards me, arms outstretched. "How did it go?"

I clenched my jaw as he brought me to his chest, his body pressed against mine. My skin grew hot with anger and my stomach turned with disgust, but the tranquilizer slowly quelled my hatred.

He hadn't really cheated on me, had he?

Robert took me home and made me spaghetti, just like he had last night. Except last night never happened.

The next day was a normal Saturday. I had coffee with Meredith as she told me about a new guy she met. On Sunday I had dinner with Robert and his parents. Monday I nodded at Mr. Bradford's requests and listened to Erica complain about her yearly review. Friday Robert took me out for my birthday and proposed.

My life felt meaningless. Trivial and petty. These people I once loved no longer felt real. Their lives were useless, filled with made-up milestones to give the illusion that life was moving forward. That they were making progress.

I could no longer pretend to enjoy it, so I left. I don't have a destination. Instead, I'm letting my short life roll over me like the waves of an ocean. Massive and unknowable. It doesn't matter where I am or where I end up. It's all so permeable. All so temporary. Why bother clinging to something when it's not really yours to begin with. And yet the questions still run through my mind.

What was something bad that happened to you today?

Nothing. Nothing bad happens anymore. Nothing happens anymore. Life passes. I exist. I question reality and then find I'm too tired to care.

What was something good that happened to you today?

Nothing. Objectively, nothing good has ever happened to me. It's all a farce. Life is just a series of signals that our mind misinterprets as something organized and purposeful. And yet we run forward with abandonment, counting the seconds until there are no seconds left to count.

Tonight I've found myself somewhere in Pennsylvania. The red numbers of the clock illuminated. It's six pm.

The sky is a beautiful amber above the mountain tops.

On a scale of 1-10, with 1 being the least, how appreciative are you of what you have?

No longer applicable

My Dog, Julie

Ilive alone. Well, not entirely alone. It's always been just me and my dog, Julie. Julie is a good dog. She came into my life about seven years ago, when my mom's neighbor's Jack Russell had a litter of puppies. I had been visiting home during winter break since I was still in college at the time. Mrs. Harris, my mom's longtime neighbor, invited us over one day to meet the newborns.

Mom had been joking all month, long before I had even packed, about how I was going to be returning home with a little one. And damn if she wasn't right.

Walking into Mrs. Harris' large kitchen, we were greeted by a cacophony of small yips and squeaks. They were absolutely adorable. There were six puppies in total: five boys and one girl. Three of them had been sleeping in a pile in the corner of the makeshift den, created by a three-foot-high foldable gate placed in a circle on the floor and lined with paper and an old blanket. Two were wrestling, and one was pawing at the gate.

Mrs. Harris chuckled as she scooped up the one trying to escape and placed her on the floor in front of us, "This little rascal here is an adventurer! She's not content hanging out with her brothers, no way. She always wants to be out and about." We watched the puppy clumsily walk around the room, poking her nose into every nook and cranny. She eventually tried to stick her head into an empty paper bag, which promptly fell, and she ran away as if the devil himself was after her. I laughed and picked her up. She was so small and felt so fragile in my hand. I hugged her to my chest and the warm scent of puppy drifted up to me. My heart panged with instant love. I looked up at the two women. Mrs. Harris was watching me with a raised eyebrow while my mom smugly smiled at me, her knowing face a perfect visualization of the phrase "I told you so."

Julie came back to my apartment with me after break was over. When I opened the door to the place, I was hit with something almost like embarrassment. It was a small two-bedroom I shared with one of the other seniors in my program and two twenty-year-old guys do not make the most puppy-friendly home. I put Julie in her crate and spent the next hour trying to clean up as many beer cans and pizza boxes as I could. Mom had taken me shopping for all of Julie's necessities, so I made a space on the kitchen floor for her new dog bowls and gave her bed a prime spot under one of the oversized living room windows so she could look outside.

By the time my roommate arrived home from Iceland, the apartment was as puppy-friendly as I could manage. He looked at Julie on the floor wrestling with a stuffed toy much too large for her, looked at the cleaned apartment, then looked at me, shrugged, and went into his room.

Since then, Julie and I have been inseparable. As I mentioned before, we now live alone, just the two of us. Or at least, it was just the two of us. It's mostly her apartment, but I get the bed and the bathroom and she'll usually share the couch with me. It's amazing how such a small dog can have such a big personality.

Our apartment is all hardwood floors, which is a nightmare with a hyperactive Jack Russell Terrier. Between the scratch marks her nails leave, which I know my landlord is going to flip about the moment we decide to move, to the constant clicking of her nails as she trots around the place at all hours of the day and night, it's a headache. I tried carpets, but Julie made it clear she did not approve by peeing on every single one of them until no amount of high-powered dog urine cleaner could make my apartment smell less like piss. I tried to keep the situation under control by clipping her nails every week, an activity we both despise, and I took her on long walks every night as well as most mornings. I even paid one of the students at the nearby college to come and go running with her a few times a week. She's a fit, well-exercised Jack, but she and my hardwood floors are still arch-nemeses.

I'm sure dog nails are an issue non-dog owners probably never think about. It's not really that big of a deal, it's just that taking care of them and the damage they can cause is a part of my life. Honestly, I never really thought that much about it until a few days ago.

It was early in the morning on Saturday and I could hear Julie getting restless. This happened every weekend morning. She was used to my work schedule but I, like most, like to sleep in on the weekends. I usually ignored her and slept another two hours, then I'd get up and we would do our usual weekend morning routines: maybe walk to the bagel place down the street, go for a jog, visit the beach, etc.

So it wasn't surprising when I was woken up by that familiar clicking around the apartment. I slowly blinked, my eyes opened and grabbed my cell phone from the nightstand.

6:08 AM.

I groaned and rolled over. I listened to the clicks, following Julie with my ears from the living room to the kitchen, her nails clicking on the tiles and the sound echoing through the otherwise silent apartment. The door to the backyard was in the kitchen, so I figured she had to pee.

My brain slowly began to process something that was out of place: if I was listening to Julie's nails click against the kitchen tiles, then what was the furry mass I could feel against my leg? I reached my hand down and rested it against the familiar back. I felt Julie adjust, scooting closer to me for morning cuddles. I turned on the light and looked at her. She looked back at me sleepily.

I could still hear the clicking in the kitchen. Maybe it was something blowing in a breeze? But I had heard the clicks travel all across the apartment. Nervously, I got up from the bed and Julie followed. I slowly walked down the hall. The clicking had stopped, now replaced with the sound of Julie's nails right next to me. We entered the small kitchen and there waiting by the back door was Julie.

I looked down at Julie beside me and then back towards the Julie at the door. Could another Jack Russell somehow have gotten into my apartment during the night? But then, why hadn't Julie freaked out? She hates other dogs. I stepped closer to examine the other dog and sure enough, she looked exactly like my Julie. I examined the one beside me again, thinking maybe she was the imposter, but they were absolutely identical. They both even had the same collar with the engraved dog bone tag that said "Julie," complete with my name and telephone number. I stood in absolute shock, my body stiff with confusion.

The Julie by the door whined at me and instinct taking over, I went and opened the back door for her. She went outside, the Julie from the bed following. I watched as the two Julies did their usual things. One went and peed on one of the bushes while the other began to sniff around the little fence I built last year specifically to keep her out of my compost. I stared in amazement as the two Julies acted exactly like Julie. I let them explore the yard for a few more minutes, then whistled to signify that Julie needed to come back inside. They both ran towards me and into the house. I closed the door and turned to two happy Jack Russells, excitedly waiting for treats.

I didn't know what to do. I called my mom and tried to explain the situation, but she congratulated me on adopting another dog. After hanging up with her, I tried to call my best friend Jared, but he didn't answer, so I sent him a picture of the two Julies. I thought about calling the cops but that seemed a bit extreme. I considered bringing one of the dogs to the pound as a lost dog, but which one was mine and which one was lost?

Unsure what to do next, I did the only thing I could think of: I got the extra leash out of the closet and took the Julies on a walk.

Jared finally called me later that day. "Hey man, sorry I missed you earlier. What's that photo you sent me? Some sort of new doubling filter? Do we do filters now? Show me how to do that flower crown one Steph always does online and I'll send you a great pic of my dick."

"No man, that isn't a filter. There are two Julies."

I waited for the smartass remark, but all he could muster was a "what?"

"I woke up this morning and there were two Julies."

"Umm… did you take something last night?"

I groaned, "Dude, just come over, ok?"

Half an hour later, Jared was sitting on the floor, mouth agape, a rope toy in each hand, playing tug with both Julies. "Maybe someone's fucking with you?"

"You mean, someone found a Jack Russell identical to the one I own, bought it, trained her to act exactly like my Julie, bought an identical collar and tag, wore them out a little so they didn't look brand new, then somehow snuck in here in the middle of the night to drop her off and leave? All to just fuck with me?"

Jared shrugged. "Do you have a better explanation?"

I fell onto the couch, exasperated. Jared stood, "I think you could use a beer." I silently agreed as he left towards the kitchen.

"Holy fucktarts!" Jared yelled.

"What is it?" I asked as I followed him. I stopped short in the doorway. He didn't have to answer. Another Julie was sitting on the tile floor.

Jared and I finished off the beer I had in the fridge and eventually turned to the bottle of tequila under my sink, trying to wash out the weird and figure out what the hell could be happening to me and my dog. We passed out at about 4:00 AM, Jared on the couch and me in my bed, fully clothed.

"What the fuck!?" Jared's voice woke me a few hours later. I ran out of the room to see him throw one of the dogs from the couch. Julie hit the wall with a loud cry.

"Dude, what the hell are you doing?" I yelled as I ran to her. She got up, dazed but unharmed.

"She was attacking me! Look!" He pulled his shirt down to reveal a fresh bite wound on his chest.

"Jesus!" I yelled. I looked down at the Julie, who had joined her sisters in the dog bed in the corner. "Fuck man, I'm sorry. Here, let's clean you up." I applied some ointment on the mark in the bathroom and bandaged it up as he told me what happened.

"I felt her on top of me, nothing out of the ordinary, so I started petting her and she fucking, she fucking bit me!" Jared said, his voice filled with venom. "Fuck man, you need to get rid of these hell beasts."

"I can't! You know that Jared. One of them is my Julie and I can't get rid of her!"

"Well, figure out which one is her and fast, man. 'Cause fuck those things." He grabbed his shit and left, slamming the door behind him.

I woke up the next morning, my head pounding. It wasn't the first Sunday I woke up feeling like this but it was the first Sunday I woke up with three Jack Russells in my bed, all snoring heavily.

Jared called me a little after two in the afternoon. He sounded less sore than he had when he left. "So…" he started, hesitantly, "any more Julies since last night?"

"Nope." I answered, "Looks like we've still got just the three."

"Well, I guess three Julies isn't the worst thing ever. Just make sure they don't become more violent, man. That was fucked up, what happened last night. And let me know if any more of those things pop up. Three is plenty."

Nothing too interesting happened Sunday, other than the obvious three identical dogs problem. There wasn't really much I could do, so I walked them as I would normally. I fed them, cleaned up Saturday's beer cans, and watched some much-needed television as a mental cleanse.

I woke up on Monday morning at 7:30 AM. I groaned as I looked at the clock. I had somehow slept through not only my first alarm but also my "just in case" alarm set for 6:45. I quickly took a shower, let the dogs out to do their business, and ran out to catch the 8:15 AM bus. I felt bad for not giving Julie her normal morning walk around the block, but it happens.

I came home at around 5:45 PM. At first, I thought I had been robbed. Everything I owned was either broken, on the floor, or both. The couch had been torn apart, stuffing thrown about wildly. Even my blankets and pillows were shredded. The three Julies greeted me as if nothing was out of the ordinary, but all I could do was stand there in a dumb stupor. I felt small paws on my legs as the dogs began to feel neglected and looked down to the same sweet joyous face I usually came home to, just multiplied by three.

I clenched my teeth and walked to the back door to let them out. I had wanted to take them to the beach before dinner but it looked like now I had to clean up. I quickly took some photos of the damage and sent them to Jared. An hour later, he showed up at the door with a twelve-pack and a broom.

Jared wasn't really what you'd call a put-together guy. He probably drank a little too much and stayed out a little too late, but he was good people. He worked the day shift at a bar downtown for not a whole lot of money, but he could afford rent and beer and was happy. My mom even liked him the few times I brought him home with me for a weekend. He was my best friend. Day or night, no matter the issue, I knew he'd be there for me.

We put the apartment back together as much as we could and ordered pizza. As we drank and ate, Jared eyed the three terriers with suspicion before finally turning to me.

"Fuck man, you need to figure this out. Why don't we mark them or something, so you can tell them apart, and then once we figure out which two are the demons, you can like... " He trailed off as he stared at me, unable to finish the sentence. I sighed. He was right.

"Oh shit, I know what we can do!" I said, jumping from the couch and running to the bedroom. I opened the closet door and began rummaging in some of the old boxes on the floor. Somewhere in there, I knew I had a box of shit my exes had left behind. One of them, Lilly, had been an artist, and I was pretty sure she left some of her stuff.

"Aha!" I exclaimed as I grabbed three tubes of acrylic paint and ran back into the living room. Jared and I rounded up the terriers and with my finger I marked each one right above the shoulder blades where I would normally apply tick medicine. I explained to Jared it was so they couldn't lick it. Once we were done, I stepped back to admire our work. In front of us were three Julies: one was marked blue, one yellow, and one red. I beamed with pride at our ingenuity. It was a pretty good idea, especially considering two drunk guys came up with it.

"Now we can try to catch the mischievous ones in the act and then…" I trailed off for a moment, much like Jared had before "and then we'll figure out the next step when we get to it."

Jared nodded in agreement. "I think you should call out of work tomorrow, spend the day getting to the bottom of this."

"Yeah, I think you're right."

"Great!" Jared smiled broadly, "Then it's tequila time!" He got up and went into the kitchen while I wrote my boss a quick email explaining that I was still up with a nasty case of food poisoning and didn't think I'd make it in.

At about 2:00 or 3:00 AM, Jared passed out on the couch so I went into my bedroom.

I woke up a few hours later to whining. My head was still foggy with alcohol but I could hear it clearly from somewhere deep in the apartment. I walked out and followed the noise to the kitchen where the three Julies were all whining at the back door. I opened it and they ran out. Since I had a few minutes before they'd finish their business, I went about pouring myself a glass of water and taking some Advil and a sleeping pill -- just a little something to try and put off tomorrow's hangover.

I was interrupted by screaming from outside accompanied by barks and growls. Not a human scream, but an animal one.

I started towards the door. My heart pounding as I imagined the two imposter Julies attacking the real one, the one I couldn't yet identify. As I lunged for the door in my inebriated state, I tripped on a dog bone and fell, hitting my nose and chin hard on the floor. My mouth filled with the warm bitter taste of my blood as I swore, kicking the bone under the fridge. I could feel my knee sting with a cut, as well as the dull ache of bruises that would form overnight on my arms and hip.

Pushing myself off of the floor, the commotion outside stopped. "Oh fuck, no no no" I pleaded as I swung the door opened and stepped into the backyard.

The circle of light from the outside bulb only stretched a few feet from the door. I squinted against the darkness and saw in the middle of the yard, a few feet from the end of the light, the three Julies standing together. In between them lay a brown mass. I limped over to them.

The Julies didn't move as I approached, their eyes never leaving the mass. I knelt down, and pulled my phone out of my back pocket, turning on the light to get a better look. The clones of my dog, and my dog -- whichever one she was -- were all staring at a dead rabbit. Not just a dead rabbit, though. A mutilated rabbit. Its throat had been pulled out and was lying in front of it on the ground, a gaping hole left between the thing's head and its shoulders. One of its legs was completely detached as well and pieces of its back and stomach had been pulled apart.

Bile tickled the back of my throat and I turned away, the grotesque image seared into my brain. I shone my phone's light at each Julie in turn. They all had blood around their mouths and necks. I recoiled and jogged, as well as I could, back to the house.

Julie and I had gone hunting a few times together, turkeys mostly, and I had never seen her display such anger and violence towards another animal before. My stomach lurched as I thought about it. How could all three be covered in blood? Maybe the two duplicates could have done this, but never the sweet dog I raised from a puppy.

I found some old gardening gloves and a shovel and transferred the semi-dismembered rabbit into a plastic bag and into the trash outside. I then hosed off the Julies, something none of them were too thrilled about, but I didn't want them in my house covered in blood.

About an hour and a half after I had first been awoken, I walked back towards my bedroom, utterly exhausted. I looked down at Jared on the couch. He was sleeping on his side, snoring heavily, the mostly empty tequila bottle dangling from his hand. He was so out, he hadn't moved an inch during that whole commotion. I laid back down on my bed, my stomach turning with nausea and my head spinning, and closed my eyes.

Sun streamed through my eyelids, and I forced them open. I looked at my phone, it was almost noon. I stretched and wondered if Jared would be up and would want to go grab some breakfast at the diner or something. I pushed the tattered blanket off of me and stood stiffly. Passing the couch on my way to the bathroom, I could tell Jared still hadn't budged. I took a piss, then walked back. I shook him. The tequila bottle still in his hand fell to the floor.

"Dude, wake up." I shook him again, harder this time. Jared's shoulder slid from beneath him and gravity forced him onto his back.

I think I might have screamed, but I honestly don't remember. Jared's dead eyes stared up at me in horror, bulging from their sockets. Much like the rabbit, his throat had been torn out. He wouldn't have been able to scream for long. I thought back to my sleeping pill. That combined with alcohol, I was the only one who could've helped him, but I was dead to the world.

His lips had been chewed off of his face, his tongue lolling out of the wide hole, purple and swollen with the loss of circulation.

My eyes trailed down from the grotesque image of my best friend's face to his chest. His shirt was ripped where the Julies had torn with their teeth and claws at his flesh, exposing muscle, organs, and in some places even bone. His entrails lay in a heap on the floor, half-eaten.

I wretched behind the couch. I wiped my mouth and my hand came away red from my tears mixing with the dried blood of my nose from last night. I heard the clicking of tiny toenails behind me and I turned to see the three dogs coming towards me. Their paint marks had been washed away last night from the hose and all three were covered head to toe in blood. I knelt before them, openly weeping. As all three Jack Russells came to me, one nuzzling my hand as another curled next to my leg, the third resting her front paws on my thighs so she could lick the tears and blood from my cheek, I finally realized my Julie was gone. I don't know if she was replaced by these three, or if she became one of them, but these dogs were all I had now.

After the shock faded, I dulled my senses with a few shots of tequila, pulled out the gardening gloves I had used for the rabbit, and cleaned up Jared's body, wrapping him in some blankets. I hosed off the dogs and cleaned the couch as thoroughly as I could.

I know you're probably judging me for not calling the police, but I love Julie. If you've ever owned a dog, you should understand. I can't let them kill her, any of them, for killing Jared. Julie is my dog and she's my responsibility.

At about midnight, I grabbed my shovel and went out into my backyard. Luckily, I live in a fairly rural area, so I didn't have to worry too much about neighbors. Still, I wore all black and left all the lights off. I went into the fenced-in compost area and dug a hole for Jared. It took hours, but once I finished, I dragged him outside and buried him.

I took a shower. I didn't even touch the knob for cold water but instead, let the hot water scald me as I scrubbed myself raw. Death and violence had seeped deep into my skin. I scrubbed until my flesh was blistering and peeling in the steamy shower before I gave up, dried myself off, and went into the living room.

I smiled down at the Julies as they wrestled on the couch. You would never be able to tell they were evil. They rolled around, growling playfully as they nipped at each other's legs.

They looked so normal.

All four of them.

The Black

TW: See Trigger Warning Appendix

I've never liked hospitals. They feel dirty. All the supposedly white surfaces permanently stained a dull brownish-yellow from age, bodily fluids, illness, and death.

Yesterday, I decided to clean out my attic. I have the unfortunate destiny of being a pack rat, like my dad, and a minimalist neat freak, like my mom. This dynamic of their vastly different lifestyles would converge like water and oil, never mixing but instead bumping up against each other. Frustrated with the inevitable resistance from the other side, they would fight while I turned up the small television in the living room in an attempt to drown them out.

However, when those opposing forces exist within the same person, there is no way to release that friction. After hours or days, my parents would come up with a compromise. My father would promise to get rid of some stuff and my mother would buy a new bookcase or other organization system to try and sort his mess and make the house more livable for everyone. I, however, have a mental breakdown that involves throwing everything I own onto the floor and then reshelving each item in what my delusional mind convinces me is a better way. My love of stuff and my hate of clutter trying to live at peace with compromises for no one. Some days I'll wake and feel as if I am going to suffocate under all my stuff. Some days I wake up and relish the full and interesting life around me, how each item and book tells a story completely unique to me.

Cleaning out the attic has always been my least favorite household chore. I take spring cleaning very seriously and so it needed to be done.

The attic is my stuff's safe space. A place where odds and ends that don't fit neatly on my shelves can still have a home. Yet walking up into that cluttered, dusty, filled-to-the-brim space still always makes my heart feel heavy and claustrophobic.

I took a deep breath and exhaled, reminding myself that once I started working, I'd get in the groove and feel better.

An hour later I groaned against the strain of lifting a heavy box of books and moving it to my large tower of 'must keep' boxes. You never throw out books.

The box dropped with a heavy thud and I heard a smaller crash behind it. Craning my neck, I saw a worn pale green book face down on the dusty floor. I immediately recognized the tear on the top right corner of the cover and the large crease at the bottom. It was my cherished copy of The Perks of Being a Wallflower.

I reached for the dropped artifact from my youth then stopped, hovering just inches from its cover. At the side of the attic, where the roof meets the floor, was a large black mass. I stayed there hand extended, mouth agape, staring at it.

The black, whatever it was, was inherently disturbing. It didn't look like mold, at least not any I knew of. The blackness was clumped together as if it was simultaneously one organism and made up of hundreds of individual pieces. Sort of like used coffee grounds spilled on the floor, somehow simultaneously dry and wet. And it looked like it was moving.

I shuddered and grabbed the book, holding it to my chest protectively. The black looked almost like a swarm of ants. It seemed to have the illusion of moving, without actually moving.

I bent over to get a better look, letting my face hover above it as close as I felt comfortable. No matter how I looked at it the black mass looked the same. Wet but dry, moving but not. I crinkled my nose and began to back away, wondering how on earth I would clean it up when I heard a sucking noise like someone slurping the last remnants of soda through a straw. I looked around trying to find the source before realizing that it was coming from the black mass.

I realized with horror that it wasn't just making a sound, I could feel suction dragging me closer and closer to the blackness. I tried to pull away but the force was too strong. I cried out, attempting to throw myself backwards, but my face and body were being drawn down. I screamed as it grew to encompass my entire vision. Soon everything was black and grainy and damp. I tried to scream but the sound was lost.

Then, total darkness. The blackness filled my mouth and my lungs yet did not suffocate me. I tried to blink but I could no longer tell when my eyes were closed and when they were opened. My existence felt heavy and thick like I was wrapped in blankets that were being absorbed into my very being.

And then suddenly it stopped.

Stunned, I blinked at the blinding lights above me. I was standing in the waiting room of a hospital. It looked vaguely familiar but I brushed off the feeling of deja vu assuming it just looked like any other hospital.

"What room is Heather Mitchell in?" My stomach dropped. It was unmistakably the voice of my mother. I turned towards the nurses' station and saw to my amazement that it was, in fact, my mom. The woman who birthed and raised me. The woman who died two years ago from cancer.

Yet, she didn't look like the woman whose hand I held day and night in that hospital, her grey frizzy hair barely contained in the elastic at the back of her neck, her ice-blue eyes faded with illness and exhaustion.

She looked upset but healthy. Not like that long year through chemotherapy. I stared at her, tears welling up in my eyes. I went to take a step towards her when I saw the young girl standing at her side, the top of her head barely reaching my mother's ribcage.

It was me. It was me when I was a preteen. My face stained white with tears, my cheeks damp.

It was then that I realized why the hospital looked so familiar. It was the hospital my grandmother died in when I was twelve almost twenty-four years ago.

I remembered this day. The day my grandmother passed away. I watched my mother and I walk into room 802, hearts heavy with the knowledge of the inevitable. I stared at the door, dumbstruck. How could this be? How could I be here?

Like a flash, the events of the day came back to me in vivid detail. I remembered walking into her room, the bodily smell of age mixed with Lysol, shit, and bleach assaulting my nostrils. My grandmother was lying on the bed, her eyes opened a sliver, her grey pupils staring up at the ceiling unaware of the two people crying by her bedside.

I looked down at the book in my hands. The novel that was given to me on this day by a stranger. The stories that had gotten me through the death of my grandmother, the struggles of being a teenager, the harsh truths and realizations of suddenly finding myself as an adult, and finally, the death of my own mother. The book I had received as a gift from an angel.

My gaze rose back to the door and I watched my mother leave the room, tears flowing freely from her eyes. I remembered this. Mom left the hospital room to call uncle Ron. That was when the angel came in. An angel, I suddenly realized, that looked a lot like thirty-five-year-old me.

Finally understanding, I walked towards the room. The nurses ignored me as I passed their large circular desk, busy with their own tasks. I held back tears as I passed my mom on one of the hospital phones speaking in hushed tones, her voice thick with sorrow.

Stepping into the room, I couldn't help but stare at my grandmother. The woman who taught me how to bake, how to stand my ground, how to write. I turned to the younger version of myself, who was staring at me. Her eyes were rimmed with the thin saturated red of pain and loss. I knelt down.

"Hi, Mary," I said softly.

Younger me wiped her cheeks with the sleeve of her shirt and sniffled.

I smiled sympathetically at her and held out the book. "Here, this helped me a lot through a situation like yours."

She took it hesitantly, never taking her eyes from mine. I opened my arms wide and, despite not knowing who I was, she leaned into my embrace. I squeezed her tight. I remembered this moment. I remembered feeling comfortable in this stranger's presence. That's why I thought she was an angel. She had felt familiar yet strange. Like she was supposed to be there, but also not.

"I know this is really hard right now but it will get better, I promise. Read the book." I kissed her on the top of the head and pulled away.

She looked down at the deeply loved cover in her hands and I remembered how I took care of that book as if it were precious for twenty-four years. Starting today.

I walked out of the room, tears burning my eyes. I thanked whatever God or spirit got me there. Whatever divine power who let me tangibly support myself.

It made me think about the day before. About going into another hospital, similar to this one, yellowing at the edges. My doctor's sympathetic face as she told me I had breast cancer. That, without chemotherapy, I only had two years to live.

I thought of my young self, of The Perks of Being a Wallflower, of myself as my own guardian angel. And in that moment, despite all the death that surrounded me, that cast its shadow over my past and my future, I swear I was infinite.

Trigger Warning Appendix

CHILD ABUSE & DEATH

The Miracle of Birth

Real People. Not Actors.

DEATH & LOSS

The Miracle of Birth

The Black

GORE, TORTURE, & VIOLENCE

Real People. Not Actors.

VIOLENCE AGAINST LBTQ+

The Angel's Game